IMAGINARY

IMAGINARY

by LEE BACON
illustrated by KATY WU

AMULET BOOKS • NEW YORK

Cataloging-in-Publication Data has been applied for and may be obtained from the Library of Congress.

ISBN 978-1-4197-4664-2

Text © 2021 Lee Bacon
Illustrations © 2021 Katy Wu
Book design by Marcie Lawrence

Printed and bound in U.S.A.
10 9 8 7 6 5 4 3 2 1

Amulet Books® is a registered trademark of Harry N. Abrams, Inc.

ABRAMS The Art of Books
195 Broadway, New York, NY 10007
abramsbooks.com

For Clara

1.

**There was a time when everyone had imaginary friends.
Everyone *your* age anyway.**

The polka-dot panda on a unicycle.

The green blob with a ferret for a hat.

The taco with arms made of cheese sticks.

It was a strange crowd.

I fit right in.

But as you got older, your classmates lost touch with their imaginary friends. Kids were growing up, moving on, finding other things to care about. Real things.

Until.

One day.

I looked up and realized...

All the other imaginary friends were gone.

I was the only one left.

2.

An imaginary friend is like a carton of eggs.

We come with an expiration date.

Like all the other worn scraps of childhood—the tattered blanket, the fluffy bear with the face that's been smooshed from too much cuddling—there'll come a time when you'll outgrow me.

Sends a shiver down my fur just thinking about it.

When you were little, you'd lead me around proudly, introducing me to the people you met.

But now you're eleven. And I've stuck around long past the usual expiration date.

These days, you don't brag about me. You don't talk about me at all. Not to your friends, not to your teachers, not even to your mom.

I'm a lot less popular than I used to be.

3.

I remember the day we met. You were much smaller then. Standing in your backyard, beneath a ceiling of branches and leaves. There was a yellow plastic shovel in your hands and a shallow hole at your feet. Chunks of your backyard were strewn everywhere.

Your eyes were bright and blue. Your face was smudged with dirt and grape juice. There was a single leaf in your hair.

If you were surprised to see me, suddenly, standing at your side, you didn't show it.

You grinned and said, "Hi!"

I smiled back. "Hello."

You examined me for a second. "You look weird."

Did I? I'd only existed for twelve seconds. I hadn't even had a chance to check myself out yet.

I looked down. This is what I saw:

Fur.

Purple fur.

Lots and lots of purple fur.

I pieced the rest of my appearance together over time. You might describe me as a ball of purple fuzz. Except a whole lot bigger than any ball of fuzz you'd see drifting around the house. I have two arms and two legs, two eyes and one mouth.

I suppose I *did* look weird. But then again…you were the one who imagined me. So I guess that made *you* a little weird too.

You ran a hand across your cheek, adding another smudge to your face. "I'm Zach."

"Nice to meet you, Zach. My name is…uh…"

My voice fell into silence. I was just beginning to realize something a bit awkward.

I didn't have a name.

But you were about to change that. Your eyes dropped to the shovel in your hand. Your face lit up. "How 'bout we call you Shovel?"

"Shovel?"

You nodded.

"Like the thing you dig with?"

You nodded again.

"Okay, then." I smiled. "My name's Shovel."

"Hey, I have an idea! You can help me and Ryan with our project!"

I tilted my head. "*Ryan?*"

A sound from the other end of the yard. A door opening and closing. I turned just in time to see a kid step out of the house next door. He looked about your age. A gangly boy with wild black hair that stood up in every direction.

"*That's* Ryan," you said. "He lives next door. And he's also my best friend."

Ryan came running across the yard, barreling right through a pile of leaves.

You called out to him. "Guess what! I made a new friend. He's gonna help us with our project!"

I still didn't know what this big project of yours was. And I don't think I ever actually agreed to help. But if I seemed clueless, Ryan was even *more* confused.

He glanced around. "New friend?"

You pointed. "He's right here. His name's Shovel."

5

Ryan looked in the direction you were pointing and saw—

Nothing.

Which wasn't a surprise. To everyone but you, I'm invisible. I'm nothing at all.

But Ryan didn't mind. It's like I said already: At that age, *everyone* had imaginary friends.

You pointed to the hole and explained, "Me and Ryan are digging a tunnel!"

"To the other side of the earth," Ryan added.

When I glanced down at my hand, I was surprised to see that I was holding a shovel too.

We got started. You and me and Ryan. Dirt crunched under our shovels as we dug.

Deeper.

Deeper.

Deeper.

Before long, we'd gone far below the surface. The sky was nothing more than a tiny speck of light above us. We kept going. Our tunnel plunged farther into the earth.

Finally, the ground broke open.

We'd made it!

All the way to the other side of the earth!

And it had only taken twenty minutes!

We climbed out of the hole. Brushing away the dirt, I looked around. Grass, trees, a house. That's what we saw.

I scratched at my furry head. The other side of the earth looked a lot like your backyard.

"Hey, buddy. Watcha doin'?"

The voice caught me by surprise. I spun and saw a future version of you standing on the back deck. A man who shared your bright blue eyes and curly tangle of hair.

"Hi, Dad!" You waved a filthy hand. "We just dug a tunnel to the other side of the earth."

"Really?"

For some reason, he sounded like he didn't believe you.

Following his gaze, I realized why. All of a sudden, our incredibly deep tunnel didn't look so deep after all.

It was just a small hole in the grass.

So *that's* why the other side of the earth looked so much like your backyard. Because it *was* your backyard.

The tunnel was never really there. It was a lot like me.

Imaginary.

4.

Later that same day, Ryan's mom had called him back home, but you and I were still in the backyard. We'd abandoned our tunnel and moved on to more important things.

First, we fought a horde of zombies.

Then we hunted for treasure under the trampoline.

Our work was interrupted when a T. rex came barreling through the fence.

The two of us ran away screaming. Being your imaginary friend was dangerous!

Your parents were on the deck. They didn't seem too worried about the dinosaur attack. Your mom was sitting in the shade, reading a book. Your dad was seated at the wooden table. He'd covered the table with newspaper. About a dozen plastic toys were scattered across the pages. They were small, about the size of his thumb. Fantasy characters. A dragon, a troll, an elf.

A tiny paintbrush was in your dad's hand. He dipped the brush into a bottle of paint and carefully applied it to one of the toys.

When I noticed this, I stopped running. So did you.

And so did the T. rex.

All three of us were distracted by your dad.

"Why's he painting your toys?" I asked.

"They're not my toys," you said. "They're *his*."

The T. rex let out a surprised growl. He hadn't been expecting this. Neither had I.

"I thought only kids played with toys," I said.

The dinosaur nodded in agreement.

"He doesn't really *play* with them," you explained. "He just paints them. Then he puts them on a shelf so he can look at them."

This just kept getting stranger. "Why have toys if you're not gonna play with them?"

You thought about this for a moment, then called out across the yard. "Hey, Dad?"

Your dad looked up. "Yeah?"

"Shovel wants to ask you a question."

He blinked. "Shovel?"

You pointed to me. "My new friend!"

"Oh!" Your dad nodded. "*That* Shovel."

"He wants to know why you have toys if you aren't gonna play with them."

Your mom lowered her book, revealing a grin. "Because your father's a nerd."

Your dad set down the paintbrush. "These aren't *toys*. They're custom-made miniatures."

"Like I said." Your mom winked at you. "*Nerd*."

"What're they for?" I asked.

"What're they for?" you asked.

Your dad explained. He sometimes got together with friends for something called Dungeons & Dragons. Which involved making up stories about characters that don't exist doing things that never actually happened. They had to roll dice and keep up with character sheets, and the whole thing sounded really complicated.

As he described all this, surprise settled over me. I didn't know grown-ups *also* played pretend!

You approached the table. The T. rex and I followed. As we got closer, I gained a better view of the toy—sorry, *miniature*—your dad was working on. A knight with glittering silver armor. A shield was strapped to his back. The visor of his helmet was raised, showing a very serious face underneath.

There was only one part of the knight that still needed to be painted. His sword.

"Tell you what," your dad said. "Why don't you paint that part?"

You raised your eyebrows. "Really?"

He nodded and you took a seat beside him.

"What color should the sword be?" you asked.

"That's up to you."

You thought for a second. "It should be green."

Green?

I'd only existed for a few hours, but I already knew: Swords aren't green. But you weren't letting that stop you.

"See…um…the knight stuck his sword into a swamp," you explained. "A magical swamp. And that turned his sword green."

"Oh! It's a swamp-sword."

"Yeah!"

I looked from you to your dad. I could see where you got your imagination from.

With a little help from your parents, you carefully painted the knight's sword a swampy green.

"Nice work, kiddo!" Your mom tousled your hair.

"That's the awesomest swamp-sword I've ever seen!" your dad said.

He held up his hand and you high-fived it.

You were smiling.

So was he.

You both had those same eyes, that same tangle of hair.

It's one of my favorite memories.

And one of my saddest.

Because I know what's going to happen next.

5.

I told you already: Imaginary friends come with an expiration date.

But so do humans.

I thought I would hit my expiration date long before your dad.

I was wrong.

6.

When you were six years old, your dad got sick.

I went with you and your mom to the hospital. Day after day. Week after week. We sat by your dad's bed, squeezed between the machines and the monitors, the tubes and the flowers. You brought cards with you. Dropped off or delivered by mail, signed by family and friends. So many of the cards had the same words printed on the front.

GET WELL SOON!

But your dad didn't get well. He got worse.

7.

Sometimes I think of your life like a page with a line down the middle. One side of the line is labeled BEFORE and the other is marked AFTER.

Your dad is on the BEFORE side.

But AFTER...

There's an empty space where he used to be.

BEFORE, I was seeing less and less of you. It wasn't like when you were younger, when we would spend *hours* together.

You had lots of real friends. You didn't need imaginary ones anymore.

When you *did* think of me, it was only a flicker. A word or two late at night, as you were drifting off to sleep. Or early in the morning, before distractions kicked in. School and activities and friends and technology.

I was fading away. And I could *see* it happening. Holding

out my hand, I could peer right through it. As if I was smoke, a mirage, a shimmer of light, dissolving into nothing.

Each day, I faded a little more.

Until I was barely there at all.

Soon—it seemed—I would be just as invisible to you as I was to everyone else.

But AFTER your dad was gone, the fading stopped.

All of a sudden, my fur was bright and glossy again. I was no longer some worn-out scrap from your childhood. I was your friend. Someone who was always there, always by your side. You could talk to me. Anytime. About any*thing*. And when you were done talking, when you just needed a distraction...

I could do that too.

We could go *anywhere* together. Your imagination swept us away to other worlds, filled with magic and monsters, excitement and danger. These places might've seemed scary, but we both knew...

Reality could be so much scarier.

8.

Your house was filled with reminders of your dad. They were everywhere. Every corner, every wall, every surface. No matter where we went, we were constantly stumbling over memories of him.

These used to be happy memories.

Now they made your chest ache with how much you missed him.

I could see how it was getting to you. Being reminded he was gone. Over and over and over again.

It was too much.

AFTER the funeral, you found a box in your closet. A plastic bin full of old toys.

You turned the box over. The toys clattered out.

The box was empty now. But it wouldn't stay that way for long. You carried it around the house, collecting reminders. Little things that used to be your dad's.

His yellow comb.

His broken wristwatch.

His sunglasses.

One by one, they went into the box.

If this had been BEFORE, your mom probably would've asked what you were up to. But this was AFTER. These days, she had so many other things to deal with. Grown-up things. Forms to fill out. Calls to make. Visits from relatives and friends and neighbors.

She didn't notice what we were up to. We were on our own. We were *explorers*.

All around us, the house transformed. Rooms became ruins. The hall became a dark, spooky passageway. When I looked around, I saw crumbled stone walls. A floor that suddenly dropped away into a bottomless pit. A ceiling that had collapsed hundreds of years ago.

The ruins seemed right somehow. They were bleak and ugly and they perfectly fit the overall mood.

You had transformed too. Your T-shirt had become a vest with pockets for all of your equipment. When you looked down, your flip-flops were gone. Replaced by heavy boots.

You were an archaeologist. You needed the right outfit.

And I was your trusted assistant. A pith helmet wobbled on my furry head. Strapped to my round waist was a belt, jingling with tools and gear.

Usually, your daydreams were fun and playful. But not today. Today we were on a mission. We carefully navigated the ancient ruins, searching for cursed treasure.

His headphones.

His favorite mug.

More items to add to the box. They rattled as you moved through the doomed wreckage.

You came to a stop. A shelf on the wall displayed a row of miniatures. A dozen fantasy characters. Your attention landed on one in the middle.

A knight with a green sword.

You added the knight to your box.

Then you tossed the rest of the miniatures in after it.

The box was full now. We left the creepy ruins and made our way across the backyard. The box clattered with each step. You set it down in a corner of the yard. Then you went to get a plastic shovel. When you returned, you began to dig. The ground crunched under the shovel's plastic blade. Grass and dirt were tossed to the side. The hole began to grow.

Deeper.

Deeper.

Deeper.

As you dug, a memory took shape. The day we first met. The day we tunneled to the other side of the earth.

It used to be a happy memory.

Now it made my chest ache.

This time, there was no need to dig all the way to the other side of the earth. The hole only had to be big enough to fit one thing.

A box of reminders.

Once the hole was deep enough, you carefully placed the box inside.

"Zach, are you sure about this?" I asked.

You stared down at the box, at the jumble of your dad's belongings. "I don't want to see them anymore. Ever. They just make me sad."

"Maybe you should ask your mom first."

You shook your head. "She has other stuff going on."

You grabbed your shovel. Dirt dropped into the hole, spilling over the reminders. You shoveled in more. And more.

And *more*.

I watched the dirt pile up, blanketing your dad's things. His yellow comb. His broken wristwatch. His sunglasses. Other objects were buried. A tiny troll. A fierce plastic dragon. You piled more dirt onto the shovel's blade, swung it around, and then...

Stopped.

Still holding the shovel, you peered into the hole. Your eyes landed on one of the reminders, near the top of the pile.

A knight with a green sword.

You dropped the shovel and crouched over the hole. Reaching inside, you dusted away the dirt. Your thumb traced the knight's plastic visor and moved down its armored shoulder.

A moment went by.

Then you rescued the knight.

Plucking it from the dirt-covered pile, you shoved the miniature into your pocket.

After that, you stood up and began scooping dirt into the hole again. Soon the hole was full. The box was buried. The reminders were gone.

All except the one in your pocket.

9.

I'll be honest. I never expected the box to stay buried. I figured you'd change your mind. In a few days or a few weeks, you were going to regret what you'd done, and there would be another trip to the backyard. More digging with the plastic shovel, until you uncovered the box of reminders.

Or maybe your mom would notice all the things that had gone missing. Things that had belonged to *him*. She would come asking and you would confess.

But you didn't change your mind. And your mom never asked. She was still caught up in grown-up things. Things you were too young to understand. On top of everything else she was dealing with, it turns out she had a big project in the works.

She was selling the house.

One day, we came home from school to find the house

filled with cardboard boxes. Your mom led you to a spot of the living room where the coffee table used to be.

"It's just the two of us now," she said, even though I was standing *right there*. "We don't need such a big house anymore."

The next day, a moving truck showed up in the driveway. Your uncle hopped out of the driver's seat. Your other uncle got out of the passenger side. They began carrying things out of the house and into the truck.

The house slowly emptied.

The truck slowly filled.

And all along, I kept waiting for you to speak up. To tell someone about the buried box in the corner of the backyard. To run outside with a shovel and start digging.

But you didn't.

When the work was done, we climbed into the car. Your mom was in the front with one of your uncles. We were in the back.

I looked at you. "Last chance," I said. "You can still go back for the box."

You clenched your jaw and shook your head.

The car shifted into motion. We pulled out of the driveway and down the street and away from the house.

10.

The new house wasn't far from the old one. Just on the other side of town. It was smaller, but that was okay. At least it wasn't filled with so many reminders. Your new bedroom was smaller too. And that was also fine.

In your head, it could be as big as you wanted.

All you needed was a little imagination.

11.

Years went by.

You grew taller.

I stayed the same size.

You're eleven now. About to start middle school. When I look around your room, I see almost nothing from BEFORE. Your toys are long gone. You've outgrown your old furniture.

Basically, the only thing from BEFORE is *me*.

Except that's not true. There *is* one other scrap remaining from that time. It's easy to miss in the jumble of your room. The avalanche of dirty laundry spilling out of the closet, the overflowing wastebasket, the bed that hasn't been made in *years*.

Most people wouldn't even notice it.

On the bookcase by your desk.

Top shelf.

Next to a crooked pile of graphic novels.

There it is.

The little plastic knight with a swamp-green sword.

12.

The knight looks out over the kingdom from his rocky perch.

In the sky, three moons glow with three different colors. Red, blue, and gold. They cast their multicolored light across a landscape that's beautiful and dangerous. Castles and caverns. A forest teeming with dark magic. A sea full of monsters.

The knight's armor gleams in the light of the three moons.

His magical sword pulses with green light.

He pulls back his visor. Under his helmet, he has bright blue eyes and a tangle of hair.

He is eleven years old.

He is not afraid of anything.

Beside the knight stands a rare and exotic figure. There is only one like him in the entire kingdom. He appears to be...

A giant, purple furball.

The furball *is* scared. Of lots of things, really. Getting beheaded by trolls. Becoming a dragon's chew toy. But right now, the furball is mostly scared of one very *specific* thing.

He's terrified of falling.

When he looks over the edge, the view is dizzying. It's a looooong way down. A pebble breaks loose under the furball's foot and plummets down the cliff. The furball worries *he* could be next.

A burst of wind blows through his fur. He presses his back against the rock wall and lets out a quiet whimper. "Isn't there another way?"

The knight points into the sky. A dragon weaves through the clouds and the moonlight. "Should I call Hank?"

Hank is the name the knight gave to his pet dragon.

The furball shakes his head. "I don't like the way Hank looks at me."

"How does Hank look at you?"

The furball shudders. "Like I'm his next snack."

"Then I guess we're walking." The knight is already striding forward again. "Come on. We're nearly there."

The furball swallows his fear and begins moving again. One foot in front of the other.

Don't look down. He takes another step. *Don't look down.*

This situation might be treacherous, but it's just another day for the two adventurers. Over the years, they've faced countless dark omens and deadly monsters. And throughout it all, the furball has been right there by the knight's side.

That's what friends are for.

When they finally reach the top, the furball nearly collapses with relief. The knight's metal boots clang the rock floor. He saunters to the uppermost edge and takes a seat. The furball cautiously sits beside him.

Don't look down. Don't look down.

Even with the fear swirling in his head, the furball can't

help but appreciate the view. The entire kingdom unfolds in front of them. Vast and beautiful and deadly.

His legs dangle over the edge. "So, tomorrow's your first day of sixth grade."

The knight lets out a groan. "Do we have to talk about this right now?"

"Are you excited?"

The knight stares straight ahead, saying nothing.

"Well, *I'm* excited," the furball says. "You're finally gonna be a middle schooler. That's huge!"

"Let's not talk about school." The knight nods to the fantastical world stretched out at their feet. "This isn't the place."

"But it's starting tomorrow."

"Duh. That's why I don't want to talk about it."

A flock of fairies flaps past. The furball watches until their light fades.

"I bet you're gonna make a whole bunch of new friends this year," he says.

The knight turns to his fuzzy companion. "Hey, Shovel?"

"Yeah?"

"If you keep talking about school, I'm gonna push you off this cliff."

All week, the furball has been trying to get the knight to open up about school. And all week, the knight has been avoiding the topic. He would rather battle trolls or take a ride on Hank. Basically anything—no matter how terrifying—as long as it doesn't involve talking about school.

The furball decides to try one more time. "Have you seen who else is in your classes? Do you know very many—"

That's all he manages to say. Before he can get anything else out, the knight gives him a sharp shove.

And just like that, the furball is plummeting off the edge of the cliff.

13.

"AAAAAAAAAH!"

The furball barely hears the sound of his own scream over the rush of wind. His fur flaps. His arms and legs swing wildly in the air.

Everything's a crazy blur.

As he's falling from the mountain peak, there's plenty of time to wonder: *What does a flattened furball look like?*

But right when he's about to make impact, the disaster scene transforms.

The stone mountain becomes an ordinary bed.

A rug sprouts from the ground.

The fantasy world dissolves. In its place, new sights appear. A wall, a desk, a window.

The furball lands softly on the bedroom floor.

14.

We're back to being ourselves.

Our normal, unheroic selves.

A moment ago, you were perched on a mountain ledge, high above the ground. Now you're sitting on the corner of your bed. Your armor has been replaced with a T-shirt and shorts.

You shrug. "I *did* warn you."

I sit up, dusting myself off. "Fine. No more school talk."

There's a knock at your bedroom door.

"Zach?" Your mom's voice is muffled by the closed door. "Mind if I come in?"

A second of hesitation.

And then.

"Yeah, okay," you call out.

The door opens. Your mom takes a step into your room. These days, her brown hair is shorter and sprinkled with gray. Behind her glasses, a few wrinkles branch from the edges of her eyes.

Her gaze passes right through me on its way to you.

"Hey kiddo," she says. "Who were you talking to?"

I look at you.

You look everywhere but me.

"Nobody," you say.

When you were little, you had no reason to keep me a secret. But now, you're eleven. And eleven-year-olds aren't *supposed* to have imaginary friends. Which is why you pretend I'm not there. Even when I'm sitting right next to you.

It's different when it's just the two of us. When nobody else is around, you drop the act. I become your friend again. Sure, I'm an *invisible* friend. And yes, I'm ninety-nine percent purple fur. But I'm *still* your friend. And you talk to me. About all kinds of things. Sometimes those conversations happen while we're perched on the edge of an incredibly tall mountain, draped in the light of three moons. And sometimes they happen right here. In your ordinary room.

The funny thing is: We don't actually *have to* talk. I mean, *out loud*. I'm your imaginary friend. If you wanted to, you could keep all our conversations *inside* your head. Our own private chat mode.

We've tried it out a few times. You'll look at me and the words are just sort of … *there*. Like I'm a mind-reader.

But it never seems to stick. And soon enough, we always

end up back where we started. Talking to each other. *Actually* talking. The way we've always done.

Habits are hard to break, I guess.

It just feels more natural that way. Almost like I'm really there with you. But it can also lead to awkward situations.

Situations like *this*.

"It sounded like you were in the middle of a conversation," your mom says. "I thought maybe you were on the phone."

"Well, I *wasn't*."

Another tense moment hangs over the room. Then your mom lets it drop. Or maybe she's just distracted by something else. Something she's just noticed on the bookcase by your desk. There on the top shelf, beside a pile of graphic novels ...

The little plastic knight with a swamp-green sword.

She plucks it off the shelf, turning it this way and that. There's a faraway look in her eyes, like she's lost in memory.

Her thumb slides down the knight's sword. A faint smile forms on her lips. "I still remember you and your dad painting this."

"Me too," I say.

"He'd meet every week with his friends to play Dungeons & Dragons. Some guys are into sports. He had *this*." She gives the knight a little shake. The slight smile reappears. "Such a nerd."

Your father liked to escape into a fantasy world. And so do you. We've been visiting our imaginary kingdom for years now. We've explored cursed caves and battled terrifying monsters. We've hung out with elves and high-fived a mermaid. When you're there, you're someone else. A heroic knight with a pet dragon and a swamp-green sword.

And a friend who's ninety-nine percent purple fur.

Your mom sets the plastic knight back on the shelf. "Hey, do you know what happened to the other ones?"

"What other ones?" you ask.

"The rest of the miniatures. He had lots more like this one. All hand-painted. He kept them on a shelf in our room, back in the old house."

You shift from side to side. Even after all these years, you still haven't told your mom about the box you buried. For all we know, it's still underground in the backyard of your old house.

She's asked about the miniatures before, and you always play clueless. But maybe today will be different. Maybe this will be the day you finally fess up.

"Um..." You fidget and shrug. "They probably got lost in the move."

Okay, maybe this *isn't* the day.

15.

Dinnertime.

You sit on one side of the table. Your mom takes the other. There are two more chairs. One is occupied by me. The other is empty. For the past five years, it's been empty.

That was your dad's chair.

You look at it sometimes. Staring. Sharp concentration in your eyes. Like you're trying to imagine him there. Still there. Like he never went away.

But nothing appears.

The chair stays empty.

Even *your* imagination has its limits.

Your attention drifts back to dinner. Your mom ordered pizza. Half-pepperoni (*for you*), half-veggie (*for her*), and nothing (*for me*). You poke at your slice like you're not sure whether it's edible. Pushing it around the plate, nibbling at the crust.

Your mom looks at you from across the table. "Are you excited about starting back at school tomorrow?"

"It's fine, I guess." You pluck off a pepperoni, sniff it, then put it back.

I already learned (the hard way) how much you *don't* want to talk about school. But your mom pushes forward with the topic.

"First day of middle school!" she says in a peppy voice. "Have you looked at your schedule yet? Do you like your classes?"

You shrug. "They're fine."

All through dinner, this has been your favorite word. *Fine.* It seems to be your answer to every single one of her questions.

Everything is *fine, fine, fine.*

The funny thing about *fine* is, it can mean basically anything. It's a vocabulary word with infinite definitions. Fine can mean *good.* But you also use it to talk about *bad* stuff. It means *happy.* But it can also translate to pretty much any other feeling you might have.

Sad. Afraid. Annoyed. Angry.

It's like all your emotions have been squished into one. They're all *fine.*

Here are some other things *fine* can mean:

I don't want to talk about school.

I just want to be left alone.

I miss Dad.

You won't bring yourself to say any of these things. Instead, they all become something else.

They all become *fine*.

"Zach?" Your mom sets down her fork with a quiet clink. "Are you sure you're okay?"

Your eyes never leave your unfinished meal. And you repeat your new favorite word for the millionth time.

"I'm fine."

16.

Before bed, the knight and the furball have a tree to climb.

But not just *any* tree.

This is the Thousand Year Tree. It stands taller than the tallest tower, stronger than the strongest wall. Its branches stretch toward the clouds, spreading out in every direction, forming a vast ceiling of leaves.

For centuries, the tree was a prized possession of the Elf Kingdom. They watered it with enchanted potions and rubbed its bark with magic oils. They built a fortress high among its branches. Wooden walls. Bridges made of rope and logs.

Then along came the trolls.

They laid siege to the Thousand Year Tree with torches and catapults. Despite all its magical reinforcements, the treetop fortress was in danger.

Luckily, the knight and the furball were there to help.

They led a battalion of elf warriors into battle and defeated the cruel trolls.

The Elf Queen was grateful. After the battle was won, she said, "Why don't you guys move in!"

To this day, they're the only non-elves who've been inside the treetop fortress.

The place is amazing. It's safe from attack. There's more than enough space. Whenever the furball is in the mood for a snack, he can reach out the window and pluck fruit from a tree branch.

And best of all: There's an elevator.

Through an elaborate system of magical ropes and pulleys, a wooden box carries the knight and the furball higher. That's *one* way to climb a tree.

Ropes strain. Wood creaks. The elevator rises. Finally, it lurches to a halt. The knight pushes open the door.

Home at last.

The furniture has been carved straight from the thick wooden branches that curve in and out of the floorboards. The ceiling is woven out of leaves. Hank is snoozing on the balcony outside. His snoring sounds like thunder. One of his huge, leathery wings hangs over the edge.

The brave adventurers trudge across the wood planks. Without even bothering to remove his armor, the knight collapses into the bottom bunk. The furball climbs to the top bunk and settles into his own bed.

"Good night," says the furball.

"Good night," says the knight.

17.

After all the time you've spent *not* talking about it, the big day is finally here.

First day of middle school!

And you're just *bursting* with excitement. I can tell by the way you slump out the door. And drag your feet down the sidewalk. And glare at me when I try to give you a pep talk.

"I have a feeling this school year's gonna be awesome!" I say in my most enthusiastic voice. "I saw on your schedule—first period's algebra. I have no idea what that is, but it *sounds* fun!"

No response.

I keep the upbeat chatter going. "I noticed you're also taking something called chemistry! Isn't that the thing where you get to wear goggles in class? Goggles are the *coolest!*"

The walk to school is only a few blocks, but judging by your zombified lurch, it's more like you've been marching for miles. Obviously, my pep talk isn't doing the trick. But a good imaginary friend would never give up that easily.

I'll just have to try something else. I reach into my round, fluffy stomach and dig around until I find what I'm looking for.

A bowling pin.

Holding the pin in one hand, I search my fur again, pulling out two other imaginary objects.

A top hat and a brass tuba.

Let the show begin!

Over the years, I've developed all kinds of impressive skills. Including juggling.

First I toss the bowling pin into the air.

Followed by the top hat.

And then the tuba.

They spin around and around and around.

I have to say, it's a pretty amazing sight. I'm a giant juggling furball! But when I glance in your direction, you barely shrug.

Time to take things to the next level.

Without interrupting the rhythm of my juggling, I quickly snap a hand into my fur and pluck out two more items.

A high-heeled shoe.

An ice-cream cone.

They join the rotation.

Now I'm juggling *five* objects. And still—you're not impressed.

I let out a whimper. This is getting ridiculous, but I'm not giving up yet.

The tuba nearly flies out of my reach. But somehow, I manage to keep everything in the air long enough to add a few more items.

A plate of sushi, a bag of concrete, a cowboy boot, a dictionary, and a fluffy, white poodle.

I stagger from side to side. My arms move at a blinding speed. A dizzying array of objects whirl around my head.

The ice cream drips and splatters.

The poodle lets out a frantic bark.

My eyes dart in your direction. I'm hoping for a smile. Maybe some applause. But just one problem. If I'm looking at you, how am I supposed to keep up with the ten things I'm juggling?

The first to fall is a piece of sushi. It hits the ground with a fishy *SPLAT*.

After that, it's a downpour. Everything tumbling all around me. The bowling pin clomps me in the head. The tuba crashes onto my foot.

The poor poodle is stuck in a tree.

"YOWWWCH!" I squeal, stumbling out of the way just in time to avoid getting squashed by the bag of cement.

When the chaos finally clears, I notice a new sound.

You're laughing.

Hunched over, slapping your knee, cracking up.

Like my juggling disaster is the most hilarious thing you've ever seen.

I let out a panting breath. My humiliation is replaced by the glow of accomplishment. This is exactly what I wanted.

I was trying to cheer you up.

And it worked.

Just not quite the way I expected.

You're laughing so hard, it takes you a little while to notice: We're not alone.

18.

When I hear the footsteps, I spin around. So do you.

I don't know what's more surprising: that there's someone standing right behind us or that the someone is *Ryan*.

A lot's happened since that day in your backyard when we tunneled to the other side of the earth.

After the move, you and Ryan weren't neighbors anymore. He couldn't just pop over whenever he wanted.

But it wasn't just distance on a map that divided you two. All of a sudden, *everything* seemed different. A dad-shaped hole had been ripped open, right in the middle of your life. Ryan couldn't fill it. *Nothing* could fill it.

You and Ryan began to drift further and further apart. You stopped hanging out. Stopped eating lunch together in the cafeteria. Stopped saying hi in the hallways.

At some point, it became obvious.

To all three of us.

Your friendship with Ryan had hit its expiration date.

Back when you were little kids, you and Ryan were about the same size. Now, he's almost a head taller than you. I remember how his black hair used to stick up wildly in every direction. These days, it's cropped close to his head, slick with hair gel.

He used to be such a gangly kid. All knees and elbows. He's a lot less awkward now. He moves with the easy grace of an athlete.

His clothes look new and expensive.

His mouth is full of braces.

And he's not alone. There are two others standing nearby. I recognize them too. Their names are Matt Reynolds and Matt Rogers, although I can never remember which is which.

You were never friends with the Matts like you were with Ryan. We just know them from school. Big guys with big voices. Always taking up too much space in the hallways, making it impossible for anyone else to get past. Banging on their lockers, teasing the less-popular kids.

Kids like you.

At some point last year, I started noticing that Ryan was hanging around with the Matts. Looks like he's still buddies with them.

The Matts stomp in our direction. Glaring at you like they've just stumbled across a strange and disgusting insect, like they can't decide whether to step on you or trap you in a jar for show-and-tell.

"Dude, what's so funny?" one of the Matts asks.

You swallow. "N-Nothing."

The other Matt makes a confused face. "Then why were you just laughing?"

You shift from foot to foot. These kinds of situations were so much easier when you were little. Back then, you could've explained, "*I was laughing at my imaginary friend's juggling disaster.*"

But now you're about to start middle school. That's not an option.

"It sounded like you were joking around with someone." The first Matt looks around. "There anyone else here?"

Matt #2 joins in the search. His eyes sweep past me without pausing. "I don't *see* anyone."

I grit my teeth. If I could, I'd drop a bowling pin on *his* head.

But that's not possible. The bowling pin was never real. And neither am I.

Matt #1 glances at Ryan. "Hey, weren't you friends with this guy?"

Ryan's eyes move from the Matts to you. "That was a long time ago."

Matt #2 sneers. "Was he always this weird?"

Ryan looks like he doesn't know what to say.

The Matts are his friends.

But so were you.

Once anyway.

Ryan hesitates another second. Then starts walking away.

"Come on." He gestures for them to join him. "We're gonna be late."

The Matts shoot you one last glare. Then they follow Ryan. At the end of the street, Matt #1 turns and calls back at you.

"See you at school!"

It sounds like a threat.

19.

"Those guys are such jerks!"

We're a block from school. I'm walking beside you, still fuming with anger.

"Massively humongous jerks!" I pound a fist into my hand. "And what's the deal with Ryan? Like, I get that you guys aren't friends anymore. But he could at least defend you!"

You don't say anything. Still walking, your eyes stay glued to the ground until we reach our destination.

Millsville Middle School.

The street in front of school is a traffic jam of parents' cars and yellow buses. Teachers and staff stand outside, welcoming students to the new school year.

You've come to a stop at the edge of the parent drop-off lane.

Your eyes hang on the school. A frown hangs on your face.

"You've got this," I say.

You pretend not to hear me.

"Tell you what," I say. "I'll go first. If you wanna follow me, you can. Sound good?"

Still, nothing.

But when I start walking, I hear your footsteps behind me. We head in the direction of school, me leading the way. Between clusters of students and parents, surrounded by the chatter of other people. Kids comparing their summers and their class schedules. As we're approaching the front doors, an adult voice calls out to you.

"And who do we have here?"

The voice belongs to the tallest woman either of us have ever seen. Over six feet. She smiles down at you, her brown eyes gleaming behind a pair of glasses.

We've seen her once before, at last week's orientation. But that was such a hectic day, full of confusing instructions and new faces. My brain is blanking on her name.

She bends down (*and down, and down some more*) until she's at eye level with you. "First day of sixth grade?"

You give her a tiny nod.

"I'm Principal Carter. It's very nice to meet you."

You mumble to your feet, "Nicetomeetyoutoo."

I lean toward you and whisper, "Eye contact."

Your eyes rise. When you look back at her, Principal Carter's smile grows.

"I probably saw you at orientation," she says. "But there

were so many new people, I have a hard time remembering everyone. Remind me. What's your name again?"

"Zach," you say. "Zach Belvin."

"Welcome to Millsville Middle School, Mr. Belvin!" she replies. Usually, when a grown-up calls you by your last name, it means you're in some kind of trouble. But Principal Carter's tone is warm and friendly. "I hope you have a wonderful first day."

She rises to her full height again, gesturing toward the open doorway. I follow you into the school, where we join the flow of sixth- and seventh-graders. Past the admin office and the trophy case, down a long corridor and under a humongous WELCOME BACK! banner. The wide hall opens up and we find ourselves in the cafeteria.

Which is where you see Ryan.

Again.

He's seated at a long table in the middle of the cafeteria, surrounded by other sixth-graders. Boys and girls, their backpacks spilled across the table and the floor around them.

I've spent enough time around other kids. I've learned to spot the different groups that populate your school. It's not that different from identifying the creatures and clans of our imaginary kingdom.

I scan Ryan's group, inspecting their clothes, their hair, their behavior. It doesn't take long for me to identify what clan they belong to.

They're the popular crowd.

And Ryan seems to fit right in. He looks like a completely different kid from the one you were friends with all those years ago. The goofy kid with messy hair. The guy who would smear guacamole all over his face just to make you laugh.

But then…that was a long time ago.

People change. They grow up, move on. They join new clans.

The Matts stride over to the group. One of them tosses a football in Ryan's direction. Without missing a beat, he catches it with one hand. The other Matt drops onto the seat beside Ryan. Jabbing Ryan with an elbow, he points at something at the other end of the cafeteria. It takes me a moment to realize—

He's pointing at *you.*

Matt's lip twists into an ugly sneer. He says something. The other Matt says something back.

Caught in the middle of a Matt sandwich, Ryan stares at you. His mouth is slightly parted. I can see the faint glimmer of his braces. For half a second, he looks just like the awkward kid I remember, the one who helped us dig a tunnel to the other side of the earth.

That Ryan would've never put up with jerks like the Matts.

But *this* Ryan is different.

He glances from one Matt to the other, muttering something. From all the way over here, I can't hear what he's saying. But I can guess from the expression on his face...

He's talking about *you*.

And what he's saying isn't nice.

20.

We don't stick around the cafeteria any longer than we have to. I trail you through Millsville Middle School. Past the library, up the stairs. You dodge crowds of students. I walk through them. When you get to the second floor, you reach into your pocket and grab your class schedule. With your eyes on the page, you keep moving.

Which is why you don't see her.

The girl up ahead.

She swings her locker shut with a *CLANG!*

And steps backward.

Right into your path.

I shout a warning, but it's too late. You bump into her. Or she bumps into you. From this angle, it's impossible to tell who does the actual bumping. Only that the impact knocks a stack of folders out of her hands.

They drop to the ground.

Scattering everywhere.

All across the floor, all different colors. Red, blue, yellow, purple. Folders everywhere.

An instant later, you're both talking. Her voice tangles with yours.

"Oops, sorry."

"No, my fault."

"I wasn't looking."

"Me neither."

"The folders."

"It's okay. I can—"

"Here, let me—"

And just like that, you and the girl are scrambling, hunched over the floor, trying to pick up folders. You grab the yellow one. She goes for purple. But the hall is crowded with morning traffic. So many people. Someone accidentally kicks the red folder. It skips and spins.

"Zach!" I point at the red folder as it skitters away. "One's escaping!"

You look up just in time to watch it twirl out of reach.

I wish I could help, but I can't. My imaginary hand goes right through non-imaginary objects. All I can do is watch as—

The red folder is kicked again.

And stepped on.

And knocked into a locker.

And squished.

You pluck the red folder off the ground, waving it above

your head. For a split second, you look like you've pulled off a heroic rescue.

Then your triumphant smile fades. You've just noticed...

The folder is in terrible shape. Scuffed and smudged, bent and ripped. The thing looks like it's been trampled by a herd of hippos.

In one corner, slightly marred by someone's shoeprint, I can still see neat handwriting. Black Sharpie on thick red paper.

Anni Lai
Chemistry
4th Period

I glance from the folder to the girl. Anni. Her straight black hair hangs down to her shoulders. I can't remember ever seeing her. But then again, it's the first day. There are a lot of new faces around.

Her eyes land on the damaged folder. "It's okay. I can still use it."

You hesitate. Run your thumb across a ripped edge of the folder.

"Actually..." you say, and there's an idea in your eyes.

You spin your backpack around. Unzip it. Shove the folder inside. Search around a little more. And then...

There it is again.

The red folder.

Except—it's been transformed. All the scuffs and rips are gone. The surface is perfectly flat, perfectly clean. Even the handwriting in the corner has vanished.

I can't believe what I just witnessed! You never told me you owned an enchanted backpack!

Damaged folder goes in. Brand-new folder comes out.

Like magic!

Or—*almost.*

We're not inside your imagination. Here in the real world, there's no such thing as magic backpacks. The *actual* explanation occurs to me an instant later.

You just traded one of *her* folders for one of *yours.*

As usual, reality is much more boring.

You hand the new folder to Anni.

"Thanks!" she says. "I can totally get you one tomorrow if you—"

You wave away the suggestion. "My mom got me a jumbo pack from Costco. I probably have enough folders to last me till college."

She laughs. So do you.

You swing your non-magical backpack onto your shoulders. "Well, I should probably . . ."

She nods. "Yeah, cool."

"See ya."

"Bye."

Then we're walking again. On our way to first period.

21.

We're the first to arrive at first period. I take a look around. Thirty empty desks arranged in neat rows. Even the teacher isn't here yet.

You plop into a desk on the left side of the room. You've just started pulling supplies out of your backpack when a voice speaks up from the doorway.

"I promise I'm not following you."

The girl you just literally bumped into. Anni Lai. She still has your red folder in one hand.

"Is this Algebra?" she asks.

You nod.

"I guess we're in the same class."

She looks around the room. Twenty-nine available desks, but she can't seem to choose. She takes a step in your direction. Then changes her mind. She walks all the way down one row. And back down another, sliding a finger along the surface of the desks she walks past.

I've seen this kind of thing before. The pressure of picking a spot. The fear of getting stuck with the wrong desk.

Finally, Anni selects a seat in the same row as yours, on the opposite end of the room.

Now it's just the three of us.

I look from you to Anni.

From Anni to you.

"You should say something," I suggest.

You shake your head.

"Why not?" I ask. "You had a whole conversation out there in the hall. Now you're suddenly all quiet? It's weird."

You shoot me a look that says, *Shut up!*

But I'm not good at shutting up. Maybe that's because there's only one person in the world who can hear me. If I could, I'd chat with all *sorts* of people. It's annoying that you won't.

Also, the silence is getting awkward.

"Ask her if she likes her folder," I say. "Tell her you have other colors if she wants something else. There's green and blue and orange and—"

"Will you just be quiet!" you hiss.

Anni looks up at you. "Huh?"

Remember when I said it was getting awkward in the room? I was wrong.

Now it's awkward.

You look like all you want is to turn yourself invisible, to vanish until this uncomfortable moment goes away.

Sorry, but only *one* of us gets to be invisible.

Anni peers at you curiously from the other side of the room. "Did you say something?"

"Um..." Under your desk, your fingers twist into knots. Your voice comes in a nervous mumble. "So, you're in the sixth grade?"

She nods.

"Me too," you say. "What school were you at before?"

"One you haven't heard of. I actually just moved here."

"Oh, from where?"

"North Carolina."

"Do you like it here so far?"

She shrugs. "It's fine."

My ears ring with the familiar word. *Fine.* Anni's eyes fall to the floor. I'm guessing you're not the only one who can pack a whole lot of meaning into that one little word.

"My name's Zach, by the way." You wave to her from your side of the room.

"Anni." She waves back.

Soon more students join the class. A whole group of them. Their loud conversation trails them into the room. They settle into a clump of desks between you and Anni. One of them drops right down in my chair, even though I'm already sitting there.

Some people can be so rude!

22.

Your day is filled with names. The names of your classes, spelled out on doors and whiteboards. The names of your teachers, introduced at the beginning of each period. Names I forgot over the summer.

A name written on one corner of the ripped and crumpled folder that's still buried in your backpack.

As the day stretches on, I have a hard time keeping all the names straight in my mind. I carry them with me, repeating them, trying to connect them to faces and classes as I follow you in and out of rooms, up and down stairs, through crowded halls.

We're on our way to fourth period when someone calls out *your* name.

"Hey, Zach!"

The voice is loud enough to slice through the chatter of the hallway. But it's not a friendly hello. Your name is shouted like it's a bad word.

A nervous shiver moves through my fur.

I recognize the voice. One of the Matts is calling after you. When I whirl around, I see their faces in the crowded hallway.

And Ryan is right there with them.

You start walking faster, but the hall is crammed with other people. Clusters of students, moving in every direction. Even as you zigzag between them, the Matts are closing the distance. They're faster than you, used to dodging and weaving between opponents.

It doesn't take long for them to catch up.

One of the Matts brings a hand down on your shoulder, hard enough to make you wince. "Whoa, hey! Wait up!"

"We just want to talk," the other Matt says.

Matt #1 glances back. "Dude, Ryan! Tell Zach what you told us earlier!"

Ryan steps out of the crowd. His hands are buried deep in his pockets. In that moment, I'm sure I see an apology somewhere behind his eyes.

But instead, he says, "I just told them about how you used to hang out with your imaginary friend."

One of the Matts smirks. The other one asks, "Is that what you were cracking up about earlier? You were having a playdate with your imaginary friend?"

You don't say anything. Matt #1 still has his hand on your shoulder, pinning you in place. He looks to Ryan. "What'd you say his name was again? The imaginary friend? It was something like Rake or Clippers."

"Shovel," Ryan says. "His name was Shovel."

This causes both the Matts to laugh.

"So sweet!" The sarcasm is thick in Matt #2's voice. "Zach and his little imaginary buddy, Shovel."

It's strange to hear my own name being spoken out loud. My entire life, I've been invisible. I didn't exist anywhere except in your head.

But now, the name Shovel is being passed around—from person to person—in the hall.

Almost like I'm really here.

For a single moment, happiness glows inside me like a light bulb. So bright, so warm. Then the bulb shatters. The happy blaze splutters out. I remember what this is all about. The Matts are making fun of you. And Ryan is helping them.

You pull your shoulder away from Matt #1 and start to walk.

"Dude, Zach!" One of the Matts yells. "We just wanna talk to you about Shovel!"

No matter how quickly you move, Ryan and the Matts are quicker. Sidestepping a group, you accidentally ram into a locker with a metallic *thud*. Regaining your balance, you keep going, but it doesn't do any good. They're about to catch up with you when—

"Mr. Belvin."

The adult voice cuts through the tense moment like a knife. Principal Carter appears in front of you. She's hard to miss. In a hallway full of middle schoolers, she looks like a giant.

Now that the principal has arrived, Ryan and the Matts have melted into the crowd of other students.

She smiles at you. "Mind if I speak with you for a sec?"

Her tone is casual. Her face is friendly. She opens a door, leading you into an empty room. When she hunches down, the two of you are at eye level.

The smile falls from her face. And when she speaks up again, there's concern in her voice. "You okay, Zach?"

Did you notice that? She switched from *Mr. Belvin* to *Zach*. It makes her sound less like a principal and more like a friend.

"What was going on back there?" Principal Carter asks.

You shake your head and mumble, "Nothing."

"Didn't *look* like nothing."

"It's fine," you say. "Really."

"Why were they talking to you about a shovel?"

You swallow heavily. "That's ... it's nothing."

She doesn't believe you. "Zach. If those boys were bullying you, all you have to do is tell me."

You shift from foot to foot, not saying anything.

"You know where my office is, right?"

"Uh-huh."

"Good. Because you can drop in any time. Doesn't have to be anything important. We can talk about whatever you want. Or nothing at all."

You tug at the strap of your backpack. "Um, Principal Carter..."

"Yeah?"

You glance in my direction. And in that instant, I'm sure: You're going to tell her everything. The truth about Ryan and the Matts.

The truth about *me*.

But then your voice drops away. So do your eyes.

And all you say is, "Um, I really have to get to class."

A faint smile appears on her lips. "Sounds good."

Principal Carter stands and opens the door for you to go. "See you later, Mr. Belvin."

For a minute there, you were *Zach*. Now, it seems, you and Principal Carter are back on a last-name basis. She waves to you as you step through the door.

23.

Lunchtime.

We move across the cafeteria, surveying our options. Long tables filled with students. Loud voices echo across the huge room.

"Where should we sit?" I ask.

You just shrug.

After a few more seconds of uncertainty, your eyes land on an empty table. We start in that direction. But halfway there, another group arrives. They drop their backpacks, sliding their lunch trays and bags onto the table.

A frown pulls at one end of your mouth. You turn, starting in another direction. But you only make it a few steps before stumbling to a stop. Following your gaze across the cafeteria, I see what brought you to a halt.

Ryan and the Matts.

They're at the same table they were occupying this morning. The Popular Table. The Matts are laughing at something Ryan just said, smacking the table so hard their trays rattle.

Before any of them notice you, we're hurrying away.

"You know you can't spend the rest of the year running away from those guys, right?" I say.

You glance around, double-checking that there's nobody else around. Your reply comes in a harsh whisper. "What do you expect me to do?"

"*Talk* to Ryan! You guys used to be friends. If you tell him to stop, he'll listen."

"Or he'll just make fun of me more."

"Then talk to Principal Carter. She's nice. She'll understand."

You just shake your head. And soon we're out in the courtyard. There are too many other people for us to continue our conversation. It's a bright, late August day. You search the space until you notice a bench near the foursquare courts. Just one problem. It's already occupied. By Anni.

As I notice her, she notices *you.*

"Hey," she says, waving.

You wave back. The lunch bag crinkles in your hand.

"Who do you usually sit with during lunch?" Anni asks.

"Um." Another crinkle from the bag. "I'm still kinda trying to figure that out."

Anni glances at the open spot on the bench next to her. "I have space here. I mean ... if you want."

A second goes by.

You just stand there.

"Dude," I say. "What're you waiting for?"

That's all it takes to nudge you forward.

You plop down on the bench next to Anni.

"Thanks," you say.

She chuckles. "Hey, I'm just glad *someone's* willing to sit with the new kid."

"How's it been? Your first day, I mean."

She shrugs. "I don't know. I miss my friends. They're all back in North Carolina. Probably having lunch right now without me. Actually—it's an hour later there. So, I guess they're finished with lunch by now."

"It's like you traveled back in time."

"Huh?"

You stare down into your lunch bag. "I mean...when you moved here, you also moved to a whole different time zone. So, like, now your old life is happening an hour in the future."

A smile sketches across her face. "Yeah, I guess you're right."

"I think that's pretty cool," you say. "I've never met a time-traveler before."

The smile becomes a laugh. "That can be my new thing. Since nobody knows me here anyway. Instead of being that weird new girl, I'll be that weird time-traveling girl."

Now you're laughing too. "Hey, that's something, at least."

"We just have to be careful about going back in time. Don't want to cause the Butterfly Effect."

"What's the Butterfly Effect?"

She sets down her lunch bag. "It's this idea that, like, if a butterfly flaps its wings in one part of the world, it'll cause a hurricane somewhere else."

"Wouldn't other things cause even more wind?" you say. "Like, what if an elephant farts? Wouldn't that cause an even *worse* hurricane? Or just think what would happen if a whole herd of elephants let one rip, all at the same time. It could be the apocalypse."

"You're kind of missing the point."

"What's the point?"

"That, like, little things can have big effects. The kind of stuff we'd never expect. Which is why you have to be careful with time travel."

Anni points to a group of kids playing foursquare nearby.

"So, like, imagine I went back in time to this morning and stole that ball," she says. "Then those kids wouldn't be playing foursquare right now, right?"

"Right."

"Which means they'd all be doing something else."

"Like what?"

"I don't know." She thinks about this. "Maybe at this exact moment, one of them would be inside the cafeteria. And when he goes to sit down, he doesn't realize—there's mashed potatoes in his seat. And all of a sudden—"

"Splat," you say. "Mashed potatoes all over his pants."

"Exactly. For the rest of his life, he'll be known as Potato Pants."

You seem to be getting it. "So, because you didn't steal the ball, he's playing foursquare instead of sitting in mashed potatoes?"

She nods. "And that's the Butterfly Effect."

You reach into your lunch bag and remove a ham sandwich. Between bites, you say, "I still think it should be called the Elephant Fart Effect."

24.

We're only halfway through the first day of middle school, and already I've learned something new.

The Butterfly Effect. Also known as the Elephant Fart Effect. Tiny things can have huge consequences.

I think about what happened earlier today. Before the start of first period. If you'd been paying better attention in the hall, you never would've bumped into Anni. Which means you wouldn't have struck up a conversation in the hall. Or in first period Algebra. And right now—most likely—you wouldn't be sitting on this bench with her, talking about butterfly wings and elephant farts.

Where would you be instead?

Maybe *you* would be the one accidentally sitting in mashed potatoes.

Or going back even *earlier*. On our way to school…my juggling show…What if I could delete that moment from the history?

You wouldn't have been laughing in the middle of the sidewalk.

The Matts wouldn't have made fun of you.

You wouldn't have to worry about dodging Ryan and the Matts every time you see them.

But let's go back further.

Years.

All the way to the first moment we met.

You just happened to be holding a plastic shovel at the time. But what if you'd had a cheeseburger in your hand instead? My name wouldn't be Shovel. You'd be calling me *Cheeseburger*.

Makes me shudder just thinking about it.

Little things. Huge consequences.

The real world is a complicated place.

25.

The knight and the furball trudge home. It's been a long day, and they're exhausted from their run-ins with monsters.

Three monsters.

Trolls on the warpath.

The revolting creatures stood much taller than the knight, with dull, gray skin and dark, evil eyes. They hunted the knight, shouting insults in their grumbling voices.

They're lucky he didn't give them a taste of his swamp-sword.

The knight's metal boots clang against the ground. They're nearly back to the Thousand Year Tree when they hear a strange sound.

A mystical jingling.

Is it a fairy, singing its song of enchantment?

Or perhaps a witch's spell?

The knight and the furball glance around questioningly.

There it is again.

That tinkling melody.

And it seems to be coming from *inside* the knight's armor.

That's when they realize what's making the peculiar sound.

The knight is getting a call from his mom.

26.

There was a time when your mom was around more. When she would pick you up from school every day. And take you to the playground in the afternoons. And cook delicious meals for dinner. And invent games for you to play before bedtime.

But that was BEFORE.

AFTER your dad was gone, your mom was suddenly around a lot less. She'd found a new job. She was working longer hours and couldn't pick you up from school anymore. Your grandparents started filling in. It was nice to spend more time with them, but it was also *different*. They never chased you around the playground like your mom used to. The meals they made tasted strange.

When your mom *was* around, she was different too. She was tired. She no longer had the energy to come up with games to play at night. She would drift off to sleep while reading you bedtime stories.

Even when she was smiling, there was sadness behind her eyes.

At the time, you didn't understand. You had already lost one parent. It felt like you were losing another.

Your mom tried to explain. Your dad was no longer around to do all the things he used to do. To earn money. To go shopping. To do the chores. Your mom had to make up for his absence. Which meant longer hours at a job that was farther away.

Even though your mom isn't around as much, she makes up for it by texting you. A lot. She'll text you in the afternoons to make sure you made it back to the house. And to let you know there are microwavable burritos in the freezer, in case you want a snack. And to remind you to finish your homework before turning on the TV. And just to say hi.

The texts stack up on your screen. At first, they're friendly. But if you don't write back soon enough, they become more urgent.

Where are you?

Are you OK???

TEXT ME BACK!!!

Until, eventually, the texts stop and the calls start. She'll call over and over. Which is what she's doing now.

The mystical jingling melody? That's just your ringtone. Now that you've noticed it, your armor has transformed back into regular clothes. Our imaginary world fades away. When we look around now, we don't see an enchanted forest or a village of thatched huts. There are no dragons in the sky, no elves in the treetops.

We're standing on a regular sidewalk, walking down a regular street, in a regular suburban town.

And your phone is still ringing.

You yank it out of your pocket and swipe the screen. "Hey, mom."

Her voice is loud enough, I can hear it through the earpiece of your phone.

"Zach! Is everything okay? Where are you?"

"I'm *fine*." You let out a sigh. "I'm almost home."

"Why didn't you write back to any of my texts?"

A moment of hesitation. I can see you trying to come up with a good response.

Because I was exploring a magical kingdom with my imaginary friend.

Because I was too busy worrying about trolls.

Because knights don't have phones.

Another second goes by. Then you say, "I just didn't see them. But I'm okay. Seriously."

I hear the sound of your mom exhaling slowly, as if releasing all the worry that she'd stored up. She says she's just calling to check on you, to make sure you're safe. But I think it's more than that. She knows too well that the real world can be dangerous and unpredictable. The people you love most can be ripped away from your life. One minute, everything will seem great. And the next—

You might find yourself in a hospital room, surrounded by beeping machines and GET WELL SOON! cards.

It's happened before.

Which is why she texts you so much. And gets frantic when you don't write back. And sounds breathless with worry when you *do* finally answer your phone.

She doesn't want to lose you too.

27.

Time sweeps over the kingdom.

One whole week.

In the mornings, the knight and the furball leave the Thousand Year Tree and journey to a vast fortress, where they find every creature and clan from across the kingdom.

The knight shuffles through the castle's crowded corridors and settles into stuffy rooms, squeezing his armored legs into cramped desks. He mostly keeps to himself. Although he has continued his habit of sharing meals in the courtyard with the newcomer. A girl from a faraway kingdom known as North Carolina.

He doesn't know what clan she belongs to.

Perhaps she is simply a friend.

The castle is ruled over by a kindly giant. Ever since the knight's first conversation with her, the giant has offered him warm smiles whenever their paths crossed.

At the sight of her, the furball remembers the words she spoke on that first day at the castle.

You know where my office is, right? she said to the knight. *You can drop in any time.*

Their days within the castle are filled with lessons on many different subjects. In Chemistry, they discuss dangerous potions. In PE, the knight tries not to get pummeled to death by flying objects.

Sometimes, the knight's swamp-sword will begin to glow, pulsing with green light. He knows what this means.

It's a warning.

Danger is near.

And then he will see them. The trolls. Three of them, watching him with menace in their dark eyes. Their laughter is harsh and cruel. Their comments are sharp as daggers.

"Hey, Zach!" they call out. "Where's your imaginary buddy?"

One of the trolls—the one known as Ryan—was once the knight's friend. But that was in a time long ago.

The time BEFORE.

Now Ryan is growing nastier by the day. He no longer stands aside and watches awkwardly when the other trolls taunt the knight.

He joins in.

"Yeah, where's Shovel!" he shouts, laughing along with the others.

The knight's sword burns with green light. But he keeps it sheathed and continues on his way.

"You can't keep running from them," the furball says for about the millionth time. "If you want to survive, sooner or later you'll have to slay the monsters."

The knight ignores the furball.

But he cannot ignore the trolls.

Not forever.

A storm is coming. The furball can feel it.

The battle is about to begin.

28.

We survived our first week of middle school!

Now it's another Monday. Lunchtime. We're in our usual spot. You're seated on a bench in the courtyard. Anni is beside you.

I'm balanced on the armrest.

Anni takes a sip from her water bottle. Printed on the side of the bottle is a mysterious-looking figure in a hat and a trench coat. When she sets it down, I catch sight of her backpack. A button is pinned to it, big letters reading TOP SECRET. Dangling from one of the zipper tabs is a tiny pair of sunglasses with the word SPY written across the lenses.

Your attention moves from the water bottle to the button to the glasses. "Wow. You sure have a lot of—"

"Weird spy stuff?" Anni raises an eyebrow. "Yeah, I know. My parents took me and my sister to the International Spy Museum like a year ago. It's in Washington, D.C. I went a little overboard in the gift shop."

She gives the bottle a shake.

"It's a pretty amazing museum though," she goes on. "They had an actual car from a James Bond movie. And all these cool gadgets. Like a shoe with a hollowed-out part in the bottom where there was a hidden microphone. And a lipstick pistol."

You look impressed. "Sounds cool."

"After we got back, I got sort of obsessed."

You cast another glance at her water bottle and backpack. "Yeah, I can tell."

You have such an easy time talking to Anni. When you were younger—way back BEFORE—you'd strike up a conversation with anyone. The new kid in class. Random old ladies in the grocery store. A giant imaginary ball of fur.

Literally, *anyone*.

But AFTER... that came to an end.

At school, you stopped raising your hand during class. You kept your eyes on the floor in the hallway and ate your lunch alone in the cafeteria.

But maybe that's changing.

When you're with Anni, you seem like the kid I used to know. Asking questions, goofing around. It's been so long since you've been that way around anyone else.

Other than *me*.

The conversation is still going on, but something else has grabbed my attention. My foot is dangling off the edge of the armrest. But all of a sudden, it looks...

Different.

I can see through it.

Straight to the concrete below.

My foot is there…

But also *not there*.

I press my eyes closed, rubbing them with my fists.

When I take a second look, the view is the same.

My foot is fading away.

29.

Worry twists inside me. I've seen this happen before. Years ago, BEFORE you lost your dad. I watched myself fade.

Gradually dissolving like smoke.

Until I was barely there at all.

Everything changed AFTER. As I became a bigger part of your life again, the fading reversed.

The memory of that time comes rushing back into my thoughts.

What if it's happening again?

There's not much time to dwell on this question, though. When Anni gets up to throw away her lunch bag, I notice a movement behind you.

Ryan and the Matts are walking in our direction.

All of a sudden, I have something *new* to worry about.

"Psst. Zach." I lean in your direction. "Look out."

You turn around just as one of the Matts leans his meaty arm across your bench. "What's up, Zach?"

The other Matt plops down onto the bench beside you. "Who's *she*?"

He cuts a glance at Anni. She's still walking the other way and hasn't looked back.

"Does the new girl know about your imaginary friend yet? Or are you waiting for the right moment to introduce her?"

"Leave me alone," you mutter to the ground.

"Maybe you and Shovel can take her on a trip to one of your little made-up worlds?" The first Matt's voice drips with sarcasm. "A little vacation with a loser and his imaginary buddy."

This sends the other Matt into a fit of harsh laughter.

"Shut up," you say in a cracked voice.

"Uh-oh." One of the Matts looks around with fake fear. "Guys, if we're not careful, he's gonna send Shovel after us."

"I said *SHUT UP!*" You bolt out of your seat, staring hard at Matt #1.

But he's so much taller than you. And bulkier. And he has his buddies nearby.

His lips curl into an arrogant smirk. "Ooh, Zach's a tough guy all of a sudden!"

The commotion has drawn attention from others in the courtyard. People have started to form a circle around the scene, watching with excited curiosity.

You try to walk away, but the other Matt blocks your path. When you change directions, someone else is waiting for you.

Ryan.

"Sorry." His mouth is full of metal. His voice is cold and hard as a block of ice. "We're not done yet."

With the bench behind you, there's nowhere to go. You're blocked in.

More people have gathered around now. I catch a glimpse of dark hair at the back of the crowd. Anni. She tries to push through the mob, but nobody's paying attention to her.

You lower your head and try to shove your way past Ryan. But he's bigger than you. More athletic. All these years that you've been playing pretend, he's been playing sports. He's used to people trying to charge past him, to jostle for position. He knows exactly what to do.

Planting his feet, Ryan raises an elbow. You knock into him and stagger back a step.

The Matts are laughing again.

I hear scattered laughter from the crowd too.

Fear weighs on me like a boulder. I feel helpless, powerless, useless. All I can do is stand and watch.

Or maybe there *is* something I can do.

"Zach," I say. "Remember when those trolls tried to steal your swamp-sword?"

You don't respond. But your eyes flick in my direction. I know you're listening.

"They had you outnumbered even worse. Like ten to one. But you had something they didn't. The element of surprise."

One of the Matts is saying something to you. Taunting you. Ryan is grinning.

But you're not paying attention to them.

You're paying attention to *me*.

"You have to catch them by surprise." My voice is loud, filled with purpose. "Hit them where they won't see it coming."

You don't say a word. But there's a fire in your eyes, burning away all the fear. You no longer look like a worried kid, alone and outnumbered.

You look like a *knight*.

You might not have your armor or your swamp-sword, but you've battled plenty of monsters over the years.

And now you know what to do.

You stare hard into Ryan's eyes. Clenching your jaw, you prepare for battle.

Then you stomp on Ryan's foot.

30.

That's why it's called the element of surprise.

Ryan and the Matts must've figured they could taunt you into *some kind of* reaction. Maybe you'd shove one of them. Or run away. Or throw a punch.

But stomping on Ryan's foot?

They never saw *that* coming.

"OWWWWWWWWWWWWWWW!"

Ryan crumbles like a paper bag, clutching his injured foot.

A couple of seconds ago, I was worried you'd start crying. Now, *he's* the one with tears in his eyes.

The crowd erupts in hoots and shouts. Phones are strictly prohibited during school hours, but that hasn't stopped a few kids from yanking out their phones and filming the scene.

While Ryan is still stunned, you shove past him. But you don't make it very far before one of the Matts grabs you by the shoulder. He spins you around and punches you in the stomach.

You collapse onto the ground, wheezing.

I rush forward. "Zach! Zach! Are you okay?"

You nod. Your reply comes out in a wobbly whisper. "Yeah, I'm fine."

I hear someone in the crowd ask, "Who's he talking to?" But most of them are too caught up in the spectacle to notice.

I've been a part of countless fights during my life. But those all took place inside the safety of your own head. Battles with mythological monsters in an imaginary world.

This is my first time witnessing a *real* fight.

I have to say, I prefer the imaginary kind.

Matt hunches over you. "How do you like *that*?"

You rise to one elbow. Matt's still busy taunting you when you launch the next attack.

A karate chop to his ear.

"OWWWIEEEE!" he squeals, clambering away on his knees.

I let out a laugh. I'm not the only one. The crowd is cracking up.

Until their laughter suddenly ends.

When I look over your shoulder, I realize why.

The other Matt has taken his friend's place. Fury burns in his eyes. Whatever game they were playing before—

the mocking, the teasing—is over. He's not messing around anymore. He's out to cause some serious damage.

Matt knocks you onto your back.

Raises a fist.

And aims at your face.

But before he can take a swing, someone breaks out of the crowd. A blur of movement in the corner of my eye. Spinning around, I see—

Anni.

Going airborne.

She launches herself off the ground, diving like a missile. She tackles Matt with such force that one of his shoes goes flying.

The crowd roars.

Once again—the element of surprise. Nobody saw it coming. Mainly because nobody knows who this new girl even *is*. She's been here for just a week and she's already in the middle of a massive brawl. That might be a school record.

The rumble rages on for a few more seconds. A flurry of grunts and grabs, fists and knees. Until an adult voice breaks through the chaos.

"WHOA! HEY! WHAT'S GOING ON HERE!"

Principal Carter moves quickly through the mob of middle schoolers. Somehow, she looks even taller when she's angry.

And right now, she's *very* angry.

The crowd scatters. The fight sputters to a stop.

Anni has Ryan in a headlock. You're buried under a pile of Matts.

Principal Carter barks her command.

"All of you! In my office! NOW!"

31.

Principal Carter's office is small and full of people. She's behind the desk. The two other chairs are occupied by you and Anni. Ryan and the Matts are standing behind you, awkwardly squeezed between the narrow walls and the door.

As for me, I'm perched on a filing cabinet.

From up here, I have a good view of the tense scene playing out below. It starts with silence.

Principal Carter crosses her arms tightly. It's strange to see her so angry. Ever since your first day at Millsville Middle School, she's been one of the nicest adults here. But now, all that friendliness has vanished. Her glare passes across each kid in the room. One after the next. When she gets to you, you look like you want to curl up in a ball under your chair.

I've never been so relieved to be invisible.

After a few more seconds of this, she finally speaks. "I want to know whose fault this is."

Now that the silence has been broken, the room is suddenly filled with voices. A chaos of accusations and finger-pointing, denials and outrage.

"It's Zach's fault! He attacked me first!"

"Did not!"

"You stomped on my foot!"

"Only because you wouldn't let me through!"

"We were just messing around!"

"The new girl tackled me! I'm gonna have a bruised butt because of you!"

"Ooh, I'm real sorry for your butt!"

"ENOUGH!" Principal Carter shouts.

Once again, silence smothers the room like a blanket.

After another round of angry glares, she takes a deep breath. And when she speaks again, there's a strained calm to her voice. "We're gonna treat this like it's a classroom. Nobody talks unless they raise their hand and I call on them. Is that understood?"

"Yes," blurts out one of the Matts from the back.

Principal Carter sighs. "What did I just say, Matthew?"

This time, he raises his hand. When the principal nods to him, he replies, "Um, you said not to talk unless you called on us."

"Very good. Let's begin."

Six hands instantly go up.

(One of them is imaginary.)

Principal Carter lets out another sigh. Then she starts calling on people. Each kid in the room gets their turn to describe what happened. It doesn't take long before two *very* different versions take shape.

Version #1:

Zach was just minding his own business when Ryan and the Matts started bullying him. When he tried to get away, he might've stepped on Ryan's toe—but that was just because Ryan wouldn't let him leave!

During the ensuing scuffle, one of the Matts punched Zach in the stomach really, really, *really* hard. And the other was about to hit him in the face when Anni heroically defended him by knocking Matt onto the ground.

The whole thing was obviously Ryan and the Matts' fault!

Version #2:

Ryan and the Matts were just kidding around! If anything, Zach and Anni are the bullies! Zach probably broke Ryan's toe when he stomped on it. After that, he performed a brutal martial arts maneuver on Matt's ear.

Oh, and by the way, nobody was ever going to punch anyone else in the face. The other Matt was just planning to give Zach a playful noogie. That's all! But before he got the chance, Anni appeared out of nowhere and tackled him for no reason and now Matt might've permanently injured his butt bone.

The whole thing was obviously Zach and Anni's fault!

While both these versions take shape, Principal Carter listens with her hands clasped on her desk. After everyone has said what they need to say, she unfolds her hands.

"Well," she says. "That was very... *informative*. You may go back to class now."

"Really?" says Ryan. "We can just... leave?"

Principal Carter nods. "You're free to go."

You look just as confused by this news as the other students. "Um, so does that mean we're not in trouble?"

A serious look falls over the principal's face. "Oh, you're definitely in trouble. I just have to figure out how much."

32.

The principal's words hang over us for the rest of the school day. A storm cloud that could burst any minute. It's obvious that you're nervous. I can see it in the way your knee bounces under your desk, the way you strangle the straps of your backpack between periods.

"What kind of trouble do you think we're in?" I ask, during a quick stop at your locker. "What if they throw you in jail?"

You swing open your locker door (*which blocks anyone else from seeing who you're talking to*) and lower your voice to a whisper (*so that only I can hear you*). "They're not throwing me in jail."

"How can you be so sure?"

"Because." You roll your eyes. "They don't throw kids in jail for getting into fights at school."

"Well, I don't know how things work in your weird world!" I throw up my hands in frustration. "Principal Carter *said* you're in trouble."

"I know that!"

"But that was two hours ago. And she still hasn't said what your punishment is."

"I *know!*"

"Do you think maybe she's taking so long because she's trying to come up with a really *bad* punishment? Like, something way worse than usual."

You glare down at me. "You're not helping."

"I'm just worried."

"Yeah, me too."

Your locker door slams shut.

I follow you to sixth period. All during class, I wait for your punishment to finally get handed down. Maybe Principal Carter will come in and personally drag you out of the room. Or she'll just announce the news over the loudspeaker.

Zachary Belvin, for your part in today's brawl, you have been sentenced to twenty years of hard labor in the cafeteria.

The bell rings.

Sixth period is officially over, and you still don't know what kind of trouble you're in.

Once we get to seventh period—your last class of the day—I start wondering if Principal Carter changed her mind. Could that be why you haven't heard from her? Because she decided you don't deserve to be punished after all?

As class stretches on, this starts seeming more and more

possible. From where I'm seated at the back of the room, I keep my eye on the wall clock.

Almost there.

Just a few more minutes and—

I flinch when the door swings open. A student enters, carrying an office slip. She hands it to your teacher.

The teacher examines the slip.

I'm on the edge of my shelf.

Finally, your teacher glances up. Her eyes find you over the frame of her glasses.

"Zach," she says gravely. "They want to see you in the office."

33.

This time, the principal's office isn't so crowded. It's just the three of us. You drop into one of the chairs. I take the other.

"Mr. Belvin…" Usually, when Principal Carter calls you by your last name, it comes across as playful. Now it sounds like a warning. "This is some serious stuff you've got yourself mixed up in."

You don't say anything. You stare down at your lap.

"You and Ryan used to be friends, right?" she says.

"That was a long time ago," you mumble.

"Your mom says you were *best* friends."

This gets your attention. Your eyes snap into focus. "You talked to my mom?"

Principal Carter nods. "I called her."

You sink a little deeper into your seat.

"When I told her what happened, she was all kinds of

surprised. She didn't understand why you'd be fighting. *Especially* with Ryan!" Principal Carter shakes her head sadly. "I don't get it either. What happened?"

"It's his fault! He keeps making fun of me! Him and the Matts!"

"Then you should've come to me. Or told one of your teachers."

"I know, but—"

"No excuses, Mr. Belvin." The principal speaks over you in a stern voice. "We have a zero-tolerance policy about fighting here."

The conversation is interrupted by a steady electronic chime. The final bell. Like an instinct, you reach down for your backpack. Your arm freezes at the sound of Principal Carter's voice.

"We're not done here, Mr. Belvin."

Your hand slinks back into your lap.

Outside the office, I hear the sounds of school emptying out. Hundreds of footsteps marching for the exits. Voices and laughter. Everyone happy to be released into the warm afternoon sun.

Everyone but us.

"I've already spoken to the others who were involved in the fight," she says. "Matthew Reynolds and Matthew Rogers have been suspended from school for the next five days."

"*Suspended?*" Your voice hits a high note. "Are me and Anni suspended too?"

The principal shakes her head. "This was not the first violation for Matthew and Matthew. So their actions come with different consequences."

No Matts for a whole week. At least *that's* good news.

But Principal Carter *still* isn't done.

"As for the rest of you…" She spreads her hands across her desk. "For the next five days, you'll have after-school detention for forty-five minutes each day. Your first session starts today."

"Today?"

"That's correct. I already informed your mom. She knows you'll be getting home late."

The look on your face is the one you get when you've taken a bite of something new and can't decide: Is the taste horribly disgusting or just plain bad?

"Is there any way me and Ryan could maybe be in different rooms?" you ask.

"That's not how it works. You will serve your detention with Ryan and Anni."

"And *me*," I say in my brightest voice.

But this does nothing to lift your mood. You slump even lower into your chair.

I was created inside that head of yours, so I usually have a pretty good idea of what's going on in there. And right now, I have a feeling you're doing math.

Five days.

Forty-five minutes a day.

Now add Ryan to the equation.

That equals 225 minutes of pure awkward misery.

34.

Principal Carter leads us to Room 107. In case there's any confusion about the room's purpose, a sheet of paper has been taped to the door, displaying a single word in big, bold font:

DETENTION

We follow Principal Carter through the door. At the other end of Room 107 is a desk where a large man is seated in a small chair. He's slumped over, staring at his computer monitor.

"This is Coach Markey," says the principal. "He coaches the boys' basketball team. But since practice won't start for another month, he's filling in as detention monitor."

Without looking up from his computer, Coach Markey grunts, "Sit."

You shuffle toward the round table in the middle of the room. Three chairs are arranged around the table. Anni and Ryan occupy two of them. They both turn to look up at you.

Anni gives you a half-smile.

Ryan gives you a full scowl.

The only other chair is squished between them.

You turn a pleading glance up at Principal Carter. "Is there another desk where I could sit?"

She shakes her head. "Afraid not. We weren't anticipating so many students in detention this early in the school year."

Letting out a sigh, you slump over to the round table and take a seat.

"Well, then." Principal Carter moves toward the door. Before stepping into the hallway, she pauses long enough to add, "I hope these next five days will offer plenty of time for each of you to work through some things."

She closes the door behind her.

35.

RULES OF DETENTION

NO TALKING

NO PHONES

NO NAPPING

NO FOOD OR DRINKS

NO GETTING UP FROM YOUR DESK

VIOLATING THESE RULES WILL RESULT
IN ADDITIONAL DETENTION.

HAVE A NICE DAY!

These rules are written on a whiteboard. Once you're
done reading them, you raise your hand.

Coach Markey doesn't seem to notice. His attention is
still on the computer screen.

You wave your hand back and forth.

Nothing.

You clear your throat.

Still nothing.

You let out a loud cough. And this time, it seems to get the coach's attention. He turns in his seat and starts to look in your—

Oh, wait. False alarm. He's just getting a better angle to scratch his backside.

Gross.

Anni leans your way and whispers, "Don't bother."

With your hand still raised, you turn to her and whisper back. "What?"

Her eyes flick toward Coach Markey. "He's ignoring us."

"Why would he do that?"

"I get the feeling he's just as annoyed to be here as we are."

The coach lets out another grunt and leans closer to his computer screen.

Your hand slowly sinks back to the table. "I was just gonna ask if we can at least do homework. Or is that another thing that's not allowed?"

Ryan joins in the whispering. "Hey, losers! Are you *trying* to get us in more trouble?"

He points to the whiteboard. Rule #1: NO TALKING.

"Stay out of it!" Anni hisses back at him.

"It's bad enough I'm stuck in here," Ryan says. "I'm not

about to get *more* detention because you two don't know how to keep your mouths shut!"

"In case you forgot," you say, "it's *your* fault we're here!"

Ryan shoots you a nasty glance. "*My* fault? You stepped on my foot! Nurse Plunkett says I'm lucky I don't have a broken toe!"

"I only stepped on your foot because you and your stupid buddies wouldn't let me leave."

"Don't call them *stupid*! Because of you, they're suspended!"

"Good!" Anni crosses her arms fiercely. "They *deserve* it!"

With each new comeback, your voices get louder and louder. Not that Coach Markey seems to notice. He's still scratching his bottom (*still gross*) and staring at his computer.

What was Principal Carter thinking? Forcing you three kids to share a single table? In a room where the detention monitor doesn't pay attention to anything except the computer screen and his own itchy butt?

It's a recipe for disaster!

After the forty-five minutes are up, Coach Markey stands and announces, "All right, you're free to go."

The sounds of backpacks being zipped, of chairs scooting against the floor.

"Glad *that's* finally over," Anni mutters.

"Me too," you say.

"Oh, it's not over," Ryan snarls. "Not even close."

He stares at you and Anni, scorn burning through his eyes.

"Just wait." A strange smirk creeps across his face. "You're gonna pay for what you did."

36.

Home again.

I follow you through the front door. As you slump across the house, you leave scraps of yourself everywhere you go.

Key on the counter.

Shoes in the living room.

A backpack in the hallway.

It's like you're trying to shed little pieces of your day.

The last thing that drops to the ground is *you*. Flumping down in the middle of your bedroom floor, you let out a miserable groan.

"Hey, it wasn't *that* bad," I say.

Your response is muffled by the rug. "Mrphrouw."

"Yeah, okay. Ryan's a jerk. And, like, that thing he said at the end of detention? About how he's gonna make us pay for what we did? What was *that* all about?"

Another reply that gets swallowed by the rug. "Hmmmph."

It's like trying to have a conversation with a vacuum

cleaner. Since talking isn't getting us anywhere, I plop down onto the floor next to you. When I speak into the rug, my words are just as nonsensical as yours.

"Pflupt," I say.

"Durrrgh," you say.

"Bluuump."

"Hurrtugh."

In a weird way, it feels like the most honest conversation we've had in months. You might not be using words, but I hear the truth in the sounds you're making. The frustration and confusion and anger. And before long, you're not moaning anymore. You're laughing. And so am I. Both of us lying on the floor, cracking each other up with strange noises.

Until we hear a sound outside. Tires crunching in the driveway. A car spluttering to a stop.

You sit up from your spot on the floor. "Uh-oh. Mom's home."

A minute later, she's standing in the doorway, arms crossed sternly. She doesn't bother with "Hello" or "How was your day?"

She gets right to the point.

"A *fight? Seriously?*" Your mom stares at you in furious disbelief. "When Principal Carter called to tell me what happened, I thought she *had* to be making some kind of mistake. It *couldn't* be my Zach. *My* Zach doesn't get into physical fights at school."

A flicker of hope finds its way into her face.

"Please tell me this is all a big misunderstanding," she pleads. "You didn't actually get into a fight? Did you?"

Your eyes connect with your mom's. You give her a tiny nod.

"That's just *great!*" Her tone is the opposite of great. She tosses her arms up in frustration. "During the second week of school!"

"It wasn't my fault!"

"I don't want excuses. I want to understand what happened." Your mom looks around your room, as if searching for clues. Then her gaze lands back on you. "Principal Carter says one of the other people involved was Ryan. Is that true?"

Another mini-nod.

Your mom's arms cross and uncross against her chest. "I thought you two were friends. Or—*used to be* friends. Now you're getting into fights with each other?"

If only I could speak to your mom, make her hear me. I was there when the fight went down. I'm a witness.

But the only one who can speak to your mom right now is *you*. And you've gone silent.

"Who were these other people involved?" she says. "Two boys named Matt? Someone else named Anni? Do you know them?"

Your shoulders rise and fall in a half-shrug. Nothing more.

Your mom pulls her phone out of her pocket and swipes

the screen. "I'm just gonna have to call Ryan's mom. I think I still have her number."

"NO!"

Finally, you've found your voice. A loud, desperate voice. After keeping quiet for so long, your words suddenly come tumbling out.

"I can tell you what happened those Matt guys they're total jerks so is Ryan he's been messing with me a whole lot I didn't know what else to do just please please please don't call his mom!"

Your rapid voice halts long enough for you to take a gasping breath.

Your mom's thumb hovers over her phone's screen for another second. Then she slides the device back into her pocket. "Tell me what happened."

And so you do.

Once you're done, your mom considers everything you told her. "There's something I still don't understand."

"What?"

"Look, some friendships just don't make it through middle school. I know that. But for you and Ryan to be *fighting* each other?" She shakes her head sadly. "That can't just be random. Something else is going on."

She gives you a long look.

And says, "What happened between you and Ryan?"

37.

What happened between you and Ryan?

The question sends my memory back to BEFORE. A sunny afternoon. Two boys playing on the shore of Willow Lake.

You are one of the boys.

Ryan is the other.

Both of you look so young in the memory. Little kids with no idea of the dark clouds waiting for you in the future. Things were so simple then. You were still best friends.

Parents must've been there too. Yours or Ryan's. Some adult to keep an eye on the kids from a bench or a beach towel. But you were too busy playing with your friend to pay much attention to anyone else.

Including parents.

Including me.

Because, of course, I was also there. Somewhere at the

edge of your attention span. Being in the memory again, all these years later, brings back the feelings from that day.

The bitter sting of being ignored.

Replaced by someone else.

Someone *real*.

You and Ryan raced each other up and down the shore and tossed rocks into the water. The whole time, you pretty much forgot I was even there.

I felt more invisible than ever before.

And when I looked down at my furry, round stomach, I could see straight through myself. I had faded so much by that point.

I was barely there at all.

Not that you cared. The afternoon sun was shining down on us. Ryan kicked the sand.

"I'm bored," he said.

"Then maybe you should go home," I muttered under my breath.

You had a different idea. "I know! We can be knights!"

I shook my head. "I don't think that's a good idea?"

But you ignored me. Just like you always did, whenever Ryan was around. And soon, the two of you were decked out in suits of armor, racing around, waving your swords wildly.

You pointed to the water that stretched out in front of us. Willow Lake had transformed into a gleaming sea, filled with monsters and mermaids.

"Ooh, look!" your voice squeaked with excitement. "There's a humongous ship sailing this way! And it's full of pirates! They're coming to attack!"

As you described what we were seeing, it was like Ryan could see it too, like the view was taking shape right before his eyes.

The enormous ship, sails flapping in the wind, slicing through the glimmering water. Packed with pirates. Studded with cannons.

You looked at your sword. "We're gonna need bigger weapons. Should we get a catapult?"

Ryan shook his head. "I know something that'll work even better!"

"What?"

He didn't answer. His attention had shifted in the other direction. A point on the horizon somewhere behind us.

Something was speeding our way.

Even from so far off, I could hear the noise it made. A deep rumble, like thunder.

It was the sound of a car engine.

VRRRRRMMMM! As the sound grew louder, I could see: This was no ordinary car. This was—

"A MONSTER TRUCK!" Ryan squealed with excitement.

I stared at this strange sight, outrage growing inside me. "This is all wrong! There aren't *monster trucks* in the kingdom!"

Not that Ryan heard my complaints. Even here in our imaginary world, I didn't exist to him.

You, on the other hand...

You heard every word I said. And you agreed with me. That much was obvious. A frown formed on your face. "How's a monster truck gonna fight a pirate ship? It doesn't even float."

"This one does," Ryan said. "Its wheels are made out of floaties."

Sure enough, as the truck zoomed closer, I noticed its tires.

They were bright blue, decorated with cartoon fish. The tires looked like the kinds of things you had to wear around your arms back before you learned to swim.

Except they were a whole lot bigger.

And attached to a monster truck.

I threw up my arms in frustration. "This is ridiculous!"

But my voice was overwhelmed by the *ROOOAR* of the engine. The truck rumbled over the terrain on huge floatie tires, smashing through a brick wall, flattening anything that got in its way.

I turned to you, yelling to make myself heard. "I told you it was a bad idea to bring him here! He's messing everything up!"

"It's okay!" you yelled back. "He's just new here, that's all!"

Ryan twisted a confused look in your direction. "Who're you yelling at?"

Your eyes hung on me for a second. Then you looked away.

"Nobody," you mumbled.

My shoulders sagged. That's all I was to you whenever Ryan was around.

Nobody.

The truck screeched to a stop, bobbling on its giant floatie tires. The doors popped open and Ryan hopped into the driver's seat.

He motioned for you to join him. "Come on."

You hesitated.

Ryan honked the horn. "Let's go!"

Another moment of uncertainty. Then you made up your mind.

You climbed into the passenger seat.

The doors slammed shut. The engine revved. The truck rumbled away.

Tearing across the shore, the monster truck kicked up sand and seashells. It plunged into the water. And sure enough, the floatie tires kept the enormous thing from sinking. Skimming across the sea, the monster truck howled into battle with the pirates.

And I stood on the shore, watching.

Alone.

38.

That day, I made a wish.

I want Ryan to go away.

All these years later, that's what I remember most.

Not the floating monster truck.

Not the pirates.

I remember my own jealousy and anger.

More than anything else, I wanted Ryan to stop messing around with *our* imaginary world.

And to stop being your friend.

I guess I got my wish.

39.

And now—after all this time—I'm beginning to fade away.

Again.

I'd hoped I was just seeing things yesterday. That it was a trick of the light, or stress from the whole Ryan Situation. But the next morning, my condition's the same.

My foot is fading.

And so is the rest of me.

40.

I've been thinking more about the Butterfly Effect.

Also known as the Elephant Fart Effect.

Little things have big consequences.

I keep going back in time, rewinding, trying to find the exact moment. The flap of the butterfly's wings. The loud, smelly elephant fart.

The moment that sent changes rippling out into the future.

Like, for example: *What if we never moved?*

If we lived in the old house, you and Ryan would still be neighbors. And you might still be friends too.

There would've been no fight. No trouble with Principal Carter. No detention.

So much could be different…

If you'd never moved.

Maybe at some point, you would've gone into the backyard with a shovel and started digging.

Deeper.

  Deeper.

    Deeper.

Until you discovered something buried underneath the earth. A box filled with all your dad's old things. A broken watch. A pair of headphones. A whole bunch of little plastic fantasy characters. Reminders of *him.*

Maybe all his things would be here with you right now. Instead, they're buried underground in the backyard of a house you don't live in anymore.

Once I start thinking this way, it's hard to stop. I keep looking backward and wondering how your life would've turned out if only the butterfly hadn't flapped its wings, if only the elephant had held in its fart.

Eventually, this always sends me spiraling back to the same question. The biggest question of all:

What if you never lost your dad?

Because that's the moment. The moment when everything changed. When your entire world cracked into BEFORE and AFTER.

Anni would probably say that I'm thinking about this all wrong. The whole point of the Butterfly Effect is that *little* things can make a big difference. But what happened with your dad...that's the BIGGEST THING OF ALL.

I don't care. I still think about it. All the time.

If your dad was still around, every single part of your life would look different right now. All that pain—*gone.*

126

All the heartache—*erased*. We would've never moved, you would've never buried the box. There wouldn't *be* a BEFORE and AFTER.

And there would be no me.

That's something I know without a doubt. If you'd never lost your dad, I would've kept fading.

And fading.

And fading.

Until there was nothing left of me.

I would've hit my expiration date a long time ago.

41.

Day two of detention.

And you have a strategy. A familiar way of dealing with situations you'd rather avoid. Just like yesterday, a sheet of paper is taped to the door. One word, printed in big, bold letters.

DETENTION

You stare at the word. Your face sharpens with concentration. The letters begin to swim across the page, melting and changing like magic, until they spell out something different.

DUNGEON

The door creaks open.

We step out of school and into another world.

42.

The dungeon is located deep below the castle. The grimy stone walls have been carved from rock. The only light comes from torches that flicker and hiss. Flames send dark shadows trembling across the floor. A skeleton is hunched in one corner. Its eyes are pools of darkness.

The knight and the furball stand at the edge of this grim scene.

The heavy steel door clangs closed.

A grunt draws the furball's attention to the edge of the room. As his eyes adjust to the darkness, he gains a better view of what made the sound.

The executioner.

A black mask covers his head. An ax leans against his chair. A dozen skulls hang from the wall beside him.

The executioner is hunched over a table, staring at the stone tablet in front of him. He leans to one side and scratches his enormous backside.

He seems to be in charge of things around here, but he barely takes notice of the knight and the furball as they enter the room.

There are two other prisoners inside the dungeon, chained to a round table. The first is a troll. The monster turns to look at the knight. His horrible face twists into a smirk.

"Hey, loser," he says.

The other prisoner is wearing a traveling cloak. The hood is pulled over her face, hiding her eyes beneath a veil of shadow. Even though the knight cannot see her face, he knows who she is.

She is a spy.

The knight takes a seat between the troll and the spy.

An instant later, a chain snakes across the floor and wraps around his armored leg. Clearly, this is some form of dark magic.

Looks like the knight is stuck here for the next forty-five minutes. Or until the executioner decides to add his skull to his collection. Whichever comes first.

"Welcome to the party," the spy says, rolling her eyes.

The troll makes a sound that's something between a snort and a laugh. "Like I'd ever go to a party with you two losers."

Under her hood, the spy raises one eyebrow. "Oh, because those Matt guys are so cool?"

"They're cooler than *you!*" Reaching into his knapsack, the troll removes a juice box. He impales the box with his tiny plastic straw and takes a sip.

"Yeah, you look *real* cool," the knight says. "What is that? Strawberry Grapetacular?"

The troll takes another sip from the tiny straw. "I'm thirsty. Got a problem with that?"

"You know that's totally not allowed, right?" The spy points to the list that's been scrawled on the wall of the dungeon.

Rule #4: NO FOOD OR DRINKS.

The troll glances in the direction of the executioner. "Since when does *he* care what we do?"

The troll might be a revolting monster, but he *has* a point. The executioner hasn't looked up from his stone tablet once.

Time slowly drags forward.

A few minutes before the end of detention, the troll smashes the empty juice box under his huge, gray fist.

Plucking the squished box off the table, he bends down to return it to his knapsack.

The furball cannot pinpoint why, but there's something unusual about his movements. Like he's an actor going through rehearsed gestures.

And also…

Why is the troll taking so long to put away his juice box? What's he even *doing* down there, rustling around in his knapsack?

These questions are flickering in the furball's brain when he hears the sound.

Squeak, squeak, squeak.

At first, he thinks the sound must be coming from outside the dungeon. Maybe a prison guard with squeaky boots walking down the hall.

Then a movement flashes across the floor.

The furball spins just in time to spot a small gray blur. It races out of view before he can tell what it is.

A second later…

There goes another one! A streak of gray that vanishes before he gets a good look.

He's still trying to figure out what's going on when a scream echoes through the dungeon.

The executioner leaps out of his chair.

"WAAAAH!" The large, masked man hops from foot to foot like a frightened three-year-old. "A MOUSE!!!"

Mice, actually. Lots of them. All of a sudden, the tiny

gray rodents are everywhere, zigzagging across the floor, looping around the legs of the table.

The knight watches with wide-eyed shock. Next to him, the spy has jumped onto her chair.

The executioner lets out another frantic squeal.

"EWW! I THINK ONE WENT UP MY PAAAANTS!" he bellows, racing for the door of the dungeon.

Basically everyone is freaking out.

Except the troll.

He's watching the chaos play out with a giant grin on his gruesome face.

43.

The mice have all slipped through the cracks and vanished under the door.

But we're still stuck in here.

The dungeon has gone back to what it was before. An ordinary classroom inside an ordinary school that's now infested with rodents.

I glare at Ryan. This is all *his* fault. Has to be. I watched with my own eyes as he knelt over his backpack to put away his juice box. Sure, he looked like a troll at the time. But it was *him*. And I know why he spent such a long time fiddling with his backpack.

He was preparing to unleash the mice.

Now his arms are folded as he leans back in his chair, looking smug. He's enjoying this.

I remember what he said yesterday. *You're gonna pay for what you did.* This has to be what he was talking about.

Except…

I still don't understand what this has to do with *you*. Does he think you're afraid of mice? Was he hoping one of them would bite you? I don't know, but I have a bad feeling there's still some evil left in Ryan's evil scheme.

The door to Room 107 opens and in walks the executioner. I haven't seen him since he went screaming out of the room. Now his black mask and medieval attire have vanished. He's back in Coach Markey mode, decked out in gym shorts and a polo. A whistle dangles from his neck.

He's followed by Principal Carter.

She turns to the coach. "All right, what exactly happened in here?"

"One moment everything was fine," says Coach Markey. "The students were in their seats, minding the rules."

Minding the rules? Everyone at the table was talking. Ryan the evil troll was sipping from a juice box. Both obvious violations of the rules!

"And then, out of nowhere..." Coach Markey claps to demonstrate the suddenness of what happened next. "BOOM! Mice everywhere!"

"Do you know where these mice came from?" Principal Carter asks.

The coach shakes his head. "It's like they just... *appeared.*"

"Hmm." Principal Carter rubs her chin, surveying the room like a detective at the crime scene. "Then what happened?"

Coach Markey coughs into his hand. "Yeah, so it was an intense situation. The children were obviously terrified, but I kept my cool."

I let out a laugh of disbelief. *Kept my cool?* I seem to remember the coach screaming at the top of his lungs, hopping from foot to foot like a terrified toddler. Nothing cool about that.

"I carefully assessed the situation," Coach Markey continues in his deepest, coachiest voice. "My first idea was to contain the mice, maybe catch them in a box of some kind, but unfortunately there were too many. So, I proceeded to Plan B."

"What's that?" I wonder out loud. "Run from the room squealing about a mouse in your pants?"

This comment gets a chuckle from the only person who can hear it. You try to stifle the laughter, but it's already too late. Principal Carter's attention snaps in your direction.

"Is there something you'd like to add, Mr. Belvin?" she asks.

You shake your head. "No, ma'am."

She gives you that detective stare for another long moment, then turns back to the coach. "So? Plan B?"

"Right. So..." Coach Markey coughs into his hand again. "When it was clear that I could not, er...apprehend the rodents, I determined that the best course of action would be to seek assistance. Which is when I proceeded calmly— but quickly—out of the room."

You're barely containing another round of laughter. And you're not the only one. Anni is covering her mouth, but I can still see the trace of a smile underneath.

"Once I reached the hallway," says Coach Markey, "I went straight to your office to report the matter."

"I see." Principal Carter nods. "And the mice?"

"They appear to have fled the scene," says the coach gravely.

Principal Carter takes a few steps into the room, searching the floor with her eyes. The silence grows thick around her, until—

"POOP!"

This sudden outburst comes from Coach Markey. He crouches, pointing to a cluster of black specks on the floor.

"Look here!" he says in a booming voice. "It's mouse poo—I mean...*droppings*."

Principal Carter kneels next to him, examining the new discovery.

"See?" The coach looks from the tall principal to the tiny poop. "Still fresh!"

"So. Even though the mice seem to have escaped, we have evidence that they were recently here." Principal Carter nods to the cluster of black specks. "But we still don't know...how'd they get here in the first place?"

"Do you think maybe the mice were here already? You know? Living here?"

"Have you seen any mice in this room before?"

"No," the coach admits.

"What about...?" Her eyes land on the cluster of mouse poop. "Come across any of *that* before today?"

Coach Markey scratches his head. "Not that I remember."

"And then today, all of a sudden, mice just...appear?"

The coach nods. "Lots of them. I'd say at least five or six. Maybe more."

Principal Carter takes in this information, saying nothing. Her gaze moves across the room. Slowly, carefully. Finally, her attention lands on the table.

You, Anni, Ryan.

Her eyes narrow. "Would any of you happen to know how a bunch of mice made it into the detention room?"

Three heads shake back and forth.

The look of smug satisfaction has vanished from Ryan's face. Now he's just an innocent kid.

I hope Principal Carter isn't falling for it.

She lets out a long sigh. "I don't like doing this, but I don't see any other way. We're going to have to inspect your backpacks."

Now we're getting somewhere! Ryan must've used his backpack to smuggle in the mice. Most likely, there's some evidence of the recent rodent occupation. A mouse cage. More poop. *Something!*

I can't wait till he's caught! If only I had a cushy chair and some popcorn. I'd plop down and enjoy the show.

Principal Carter crouches next to Ryan. Unzipping his backpack, she searches inside.

Her mouth forms a concerned frown. "What do we have here?"

I lean forward, rubbing my hands in anticipation.

The principal reaches deeper into the backpack and pulls out...

A squashed juice box. The label reads *Strawberry Grapetacular.*

"Is there a reason you didn't throw this in the trash?" Principal Carter asks.

"Oops!" Ryan says apologetically. "Guess I forgot it was there."

"Well, you should be more careful. Don't want to get juice on any of your textbooks." Principal Carter sets the box on the table.

She takes one more quick glance into Ryan's backpack, then zips it closed.

"Wait!" I say, even though I know she can't hear me. "Don't you wanna keep looking? There's gotta be something else in there!"

But Principal Carter is already moving on to your backpack. And I'm left feeling a whole lot like the box of juice.

Squished and empty.

How is this possible? Ryan's a troll, not a wizard. He

couldn't have conjured the mice out of thin air. He *must've* brought them inside his backpack. But if that's the case, there's only one way he could've ditched the evidence.

Oh no.

All of a sudden, I understand. The mice were only the *first* part of Ryan's evil scheme.

My worried glance darts in your direction. But before I can warn you—

"Can you explain this, Mr. Belvin?"

Principal Carter reaches into your backpack and removes a bag of mouse food.

44.

Ryan is worse than a troll. He's pure evil.

I think about the chaos inside Room 107 after the mice were set loose. While everyone else was distracted, Ryan must've slipped the bag of mouse food into your backpack.

And it gets worse.

When Principal Carter searches Anni's backpack, she finds a small cardboard box with holes punched in the top. Perfect for transporting rodents.

"That's not mine," Anni says in a trembling voice.

You point at the bag of mouse food. "Yeah, and I definitely didn't bring *that*!"

From his side of the table, Ryan watches the scene play out with a look of bewildered innocence, as if he can't *believe* what's just happened.

But when you catch his eye, his mouth twists into a smile that only you can see.

An instant later, the grin is gone.

"Ryan did this!" you blurt out. "I know he did!"

Principal Carter shakes her head. "You watched me check Ryan's backpack. There wasn't anything in there that would make me suspect he was involved." Her eyes narrow as they move from you to Anni. "You two, on the other hand..."

The principal stands.

"I want to speak to both of you in my office," she says. "Let's go."

Principal Carter stomps out of the room.

You and Anni follow her.

The door slams shut in my face. Not that I let that stop me.

45.

Well, here we are again.

I never thought we'd be spending so much time in the principal's office. You and Anni are occupying the two available chairs. I've taken my usual spot on the filing cabinet.

Principal Carter sets the evidence down on her desk.

One bag of mouse food.

One cardboard box, holes punched into the top.

"You have to admit," she begins gravely. "This doesn't look good."

You lean forward. "But that isn't ours! Ryan must've snuck them into our bags when we were all distracted by the mice!"

"Did anyone *see* him doing this?"

You share a look with Anni. She shakes her head.

"No," you admit.

"Without any evidence to back up your claims, it's your

word against Ryan's," says the principal. "And right now, it looks a whole lot like you two released mice in my school."

I grip the edge of the filing cabinet tighter.

"I can see how the sudden arrival of so many mice *might* create the perfect opportunity to plant these objects in your backpacks." Her attention lands back on the cardboard box and the mouse food. "But we can't know for sure. Which is why I won't be assigning you any additional detention."

You and Anni break into a chorus of *thank you's*.

"But ..." Principal Carter says. "If there's any more trouble from you two, I won't be so generous. Is that understood?"

You both nod.

"Good." Her eyes land on Anni. "You can go, Ms. Lai."

Anni stands.

You remain in your chair. The relief in your expression is turning to worry. "Um. What about me?"

"I'd like to speak with you a little more," says Principal Carter. "Alone."

Anni gives you a look of pity, then hurries out of the room. Now it's just the three of us.

You sink into your chair. Any second, you might just slide right off your seat and melt into a puddle on the floor. But it doesn't seem like the principal kept you here for extra punishment. If anything, her expression has softened. As she speaks, there's a quiet kindness in her voice.

"When I talked to your mom yesterday, she told me about what happened. To your dad. I'm so, so sorry."

Your hands are twisted into a tight knot. You stare at your knees.

"These past few years must've been really tough for you and your family."

We both nod.

Principal Carter goes on. "Your mom also mentioned that you have a very ... active imagination. Would you say that's the case?"

You mumble something that sounds like "I guess."

"She sometimes hears you talking to someone." Principal Carter clears her throat. "Someone who isn't there."

Your hands clench into fists. Concentration consumes your face. I know what you're trying to do. To turn this room into something else. Another world, far from the worries of this one. To turn the principal into a mythical giant. To create a suit of armor around yourself that's so strong and so unbreakable, nobody can reach you.

Anything to escape from here.

But none of it works. No matter how hard you try, you can't make this conversation go away.

"Zach ..." she tries again.

Your name hangs in the air. Your *first* name. Just like on day one, Principal Carter has switched from *Mr. Belvin* to *Zach*.

You look up. "I know he's not there."

"*Who's* not there?"

"My imaginary friend." You exhale a breath, like it's

145

a relief to say these words out loud. "I know he's just in my head."

"And you talk to him anyway?"

You don't say anything for a long time. Just when I'm starting to think you've abandoned the conversation, you say, "When I'm talking to my imaginary friend, it makes me feel like there's someone else there. Like I'm less alone."

"What's his name?"

Your eyes flick in my direction. "Shovel."

"Hmm." Principal Carter forms a steeple with her fingers. "Interesting."

"*What's* interesting?"

"Have you ever thought about that name? Shovel?"

"Um…"

You glance at me again. I just shrug.

"I mean, not really," you admit.

"Well, here's the thing, Zach." The principal's brown eyes sparkle a little brighter. "A shovel is also a tool."

"A *tool*?"

She nods. "Something that you can *use*. Something that *helps* you. Maybe it would be beneficial to think of your *imaginary friend* Shovel in the same way."

"As a tool?"

She nods. "Like his name, Shovel can help you. I'm sure he already *has* helped you. To deal with this loss that you've experienced."

I scoot forward on my cabinet, listening closely. I'm not

used to being the topic of conversation. It's strange—kind of exciting, kind of scary—to be sitting here, listening to you talk about me with someone else.

Principal Carter says I can be helpful. But I don't think she means it in the ways I *usually* think of myself as helpful. Like, how I always pack an extra pair of imaginary boots in my fur when we're exploring forbidden caves (just in case you accidentally step in a pile of dragon poop).

She means I can help you with something even *bigger*. Which is saying something, because we both know, dragon poop is HUGE.

"Zach, you've gone through something incredibly difficult. The loss of a parent." She shakes her head, breathing a heavy sigh. "When something like that happens, you have to find ways to cope. Sometimes, that means going into your own head. That's a valid way of dealing with a tough situation."

She gives you a long look, spreading her hands across the desk like she's smoothing out the folds on a blanket.

"I think it's great that you have Shovel to help you," she says. "But there are also other ways of using your imagination."

You look up. "What do you mean?"

"Well. Maybe—instead of always using your imagination to get deeper inside your head—you could also try . . . letting it out."

"How?"

"There are all kinds of ways to use your imagination. You could write in a diary. Or make a video. Or draw something."

You cast a quick glance up to the top of the filing cabinet, like you're checking to see what I have to say about all this.

"I'd like you to try something like that," says Principal Carter. "Something creative. Whatever you want."

"Is there gonna be a grade?"

Principal Carter smiles at this. "Don't worry. It won't go on your transcript. You don't even have to show me, unless you want to."

She taps her desk once, like a punctuation mark at the end of the conversation.

"Well, then, Mr. Belvin," she says. "You're free to go."

46.

As we're leaving school, there's a rustle of footsteps behind us. I spin around, nervous about what I might see. A troll sneaking up on us? An army of angry mice?

Instead, the footsteps belong to Anni.

"Hey!" She jogs to catch up. "What was *that* all about? Why'd she want to talk to you?"

"Um…" You glance at me.

All I can do is shrug. "Don't look at *me*."

"She just wanted to talk about…" Your eyes drop to the ground. "School stuff."

Anni looks relieved to hear this. "I was scared she was gonna, like, make you move to a different room for detention and I'd be stuck alone with Ryan." She makes a barf gesture.

"No worries. I'll still be in the dungeon with you."

She raises an eyebrow. "*Dungeon?*"

Realization flashes in your eyes. The word must've

slipped out. You're still struggling to come up with a response when Anni breaks into laughter.

She gives your shoulder a friendly punch. "You're funny, you know that, Zach!"

"Oh. Um, yeah."

"That room totally *could* be a dungeon."

"And now, there are even rodents."

"You know what we should do?" Anni says.

"What?"

The smile has vanished from her face. Anni has gone serious all of a sudden. She glances in both directions, making sure nobody else is around. Then she leans in close, her voice dropping to a whisper.

And she says, "We have to get revenge."

47.

A revenge plot! Fun!

But figuring out exactly *how* to get revenge...

That's where it gets tricky. All our ideas are too dangerous. Or too tame. Or totally unrealistic.

"We don't want to hurt Ryan," Anni says.

"You *sure* about that?" I grumble.

"But we need to make him pay." She pounds a fist into her hand. "Show him he can't keep messing with us."

I wish I could help. But all my best revenge ideas come from a faraway fantasy kingdom. Magical spells, demon spiders, cursed catapults. The knight and the furball deal with this kind of stuff all the time. But that's in your imagination. The real world is a lot more complicated.

"Look, we don't have to come up with something right this *second*," Anni says, finally. "Let's think of it like...like homework."

First Principal Carter says you should do something creative in your free time. Now Anni's asking you to brainstorm revenge plots after school.

The extracurricular assignments are really piling up.

"I'll see what I come up with," Anni continues. "And you can do the same. We can compare ideas later."

"Sounds good," you say. "Do you wanna give me your number? That way, I can text you if I come up with something."

Anni shakes her head. "Nope. Bad idea."

"Oh." Your shoulders sag. "If you don't wanna give me your number, that's fine too."

"What? No!" She makes a *don't-be-ridiculous* face. "It's not *that!* I just don't think it's a good idea to text. At least, not about this."

"How come?"

"Because. Then the whole thing's, like, recorded in writing and stored in the cloud. You saw how Principal Carter was back there during detention, searching our backpacks. We can't risk leaving any traces behind."

"Wow." I tap the side of my furry head with one finger. "Good thinking."

She ponders the situation for another long moment. When her eyes land on you again, they're filled with an idea. "Actually, I just watched this documentary about spying and they had a way of dealing with a situation like this."

"Hold up." You give Anni a worried look. "Does this plan involve a lipstick pistol?"

She shakes her head. "The only thing we'll need is a little toilet paper."

You blink. "Toilet paper?"

"See, when spies wanted to share secret information, sometimes they would write it on toilet paper. When the other person found it, they'd memorize what was on the sheet, then they'd go to the bathroom and flush it. Boom. No evidence."

I can hear the excitement in Anni's voice. As she speaks, the miniature spy sunglasses bounce up and down from the zipper of her backpack.

"We can do the same thing!" she says. "If you come up with an idea for how to get revenge against Ryan, write it down on toilet paper, then slip it into my locker when you get to school."

You nod along. But clearly there's something you're still wondering about. "Should the toilet paper be one-ply? Or can it be two-ply?"

Anni stares back at you, bewildered. "Huh?"

"It's just that two-ply has extra padding, so it's more comfortable on your—"

"Okay, too much information!" Anni cuts in. "Look, it doesn't matter what *kind* of toilet paper. The important thing is, we flush it as soon as we memorize the information. Got it?"

"Got it."

"If I have any ideas, I'll do the same thing in your locker."

I can feel the thrill buzzing inside me. The homework you usually bring home from school is never this interesting.

This time, your assignment is to plot revenge.

48.

An hour later, you're seated at your desk with a magic marker and a roll of toilet paper.

I'm standing next to you. "Anything?"

You shake your head. "You?"

"Nothing."

Our brainstorming session has turned up exactly *zero* revenge plots. You haven't written a single thing on the toilet paper.

Your feet tap the floor. Your eyes lazily wander the room. They land on your bookcase. There on the top shelf, next to the crooked pile of graphic novels, is the little plastic knight with a swamp-green sword.

You push the toilet paper to a corner of your desk. Standing up, you grab the knight off the shelf and plunk it down next to a blank sheet of paper. You trade the magic marker for a #2 pencil. And instead of writing out a secret message...

155

You begin to draw.

The paper fills with your markings. Lines become shapes. A picture forms. When a line goes astray, you erase it and start over.

I peer over your shoulder. "What're you doing?"

But I already know the answer. You're doing what Principal Carter asked you to do. Earlier today, in her office. She suggested you find new ways to use your imagination. You could write in a diary, or make a video...

Or draw something.

As you work, you keep looking up to inspect the

miniature knight, comparing it to the drawing, adding details as you go.

A metal helmet.

A suit of armor.

A sword, glowing with magic.

When you're finally finished, you lean back in your chair and take a long look at what you've drawn. A second goes by. Then you crumple up the page and toss it into the trash.

"Why'd you do *that*?" I ask. "I thought it was good!"

But you just shake your head.

And then you start again.

The next version takes form on the page. It's the same as the one before—just a little better. The lines are clearer. The details are sharper.

But it's still not good enough.

Another ball of paper lands in the trash basket.

You start over again.

And again.

And *again*.

Honestly, how much drawing can one imaginary friend take? Leaving you at your desk, I position myself next to the wall vent.

Then I wait. Until I hear the sound, somewhere deep inside the wall. A sound that's like a sudden gulp of air, like your entire house is holding in a burp.

The sound of the air conditioner switching on.

A cool breeze bursts through the vent. I'm ready for it. My arms are tucked into my fuzzy midsection. My legs are bent. I'm curled up into a ball. A chilly gust rushes past me. And all of a sudden—

The AC bounces me around your room.

There are advantages to being ninety-nine percent purple fur. I drift through the air like a balloon, bumping against walls and spinning off furniture.

But even after I'm done bouncing, you're still at it. Working on the gazillionth draft of the knight illustration.

Maybe it's all this attention you're giving to the knight, but I can't stop thinking about his little plastic buddies. All those other miniatures. A dragon, a wizard, a troll. And a bunch more. Carefully painted by your dad.

AFTER he was gone, they went into a box. Along with some of his other things. A yellow comb. A pair of sunglasses. His favorite mug. You grabbed your little plastic shovel and went into the backyard and started digging.

Deeper.

Deeper.

Deeper.

Eventually, you dropped the box inside and covered it with dirt, only stopping long enough to rescue *this*. The knight with the green sword.

"Hey, Zach," I say. "Do you ever wonder about the box?"

You don't look up from your drawing. But I can see it in your face: You know exactly what box I'm talking about.

"Yeah." Your voice is soft with memory. "I guess sometimes."

"Do you think anyone ever found it? Like, the people who moved in after us?"

You shake your head. "It was off in a corner of the yard, behind a bunch of bushes. You'd have to know exactly where to look."

"Yeah. You're probably right."

In the back of my mind, I see that spot in your old backyard. Off in the corner, behind the bushes. For a while, the ground was probably raw. There were traces that some digging had gone on there. But time passed. Grass grew. At some point, that little patch of earth looked like everything around it.

And the things beneath it stayed hidden.

For all these years.

The only ones who know about the hole—and the things inside it—are *us*.

49.

Your art project is put on pause when your mom calls you to the table for dinner.

"You've been busy in your room for a while now." She spoons rice and vegetables onto your plate. "What're you working on? Is it something for school?"

You pop a carrot into your mouth. "Kind of."

"What's *that* mean?"

"It's just something Principal Carter said I should try."

"Like an extracurricular assignment?"

You nod. "I'm still trying to get it right."

That's *one* way of putting it. You've done at least twenty versions of the same exact drawing. And each one has gone into the trash.

Your mom takes a bite, then asks, "Do you want to show me what you've done so far?"

You think about this for a moment, then shake your head. "Maybe once I'm done."

She accepts this with a smile. "Well, I'm glad you're excited about it."

Once your plate is empty, you set down your fork. "Hey, Mom?"

"Yeah."

"Is it okay if I go back to my room now?"

"So you can keep working on your assignment?"

"Yeah."

"Sure, kiddo."

Soon you're back at your desk, leaning forward in your chair, scratching at the page with your pencil. It's amazing how far you've come since that first attempt. The picture has depth and shadows. Any second, it looks like the knight might climb out of the page and charge into battle.

You've even added details that aren't a part of the miniature.

Mud caked to the bottoms of his metal boots.

A small dent in his armor.

But the biggest difference is in the face. He looks younger.

And there's something about his eyes.

They remind me of *your* eyes.

It's getting late. Night presses against the windows of your room. While you work, I look down at my hands, my round belly, my feet. I can't help noticing—

There's less of me now.

It's unmistakable.

The fading is getting worse.

50.

The sky is filled with gray clouds, and our walk to school comes with a soundtrack of booming thunder. An umbrella pokes out of your backpack like a swamp-sword.

"That drawing you made yesterday was pretty amazing," I say. "Are you gonna draw anything else?"

You just shrug.

"What about the whole revenge plot? Did you ever come up with any ideas?"

The shrug becomes a shake of the head.

That's what I figured. I would've noticed if you'd written anything on the toilet paper roll.

We continue walking. Your footsteps skitter over the sidewalk. Mine glide silently just above the surface.

Thunder growls.

Halfway to school, you come to a sudden stop. You hold out your hand, palm facing up to the sky.

A giant plop of rain lands in the middle of your palm.

Your umbrella pops open. The downpour starts.

We spend the rest of our walk to school dodging puddles of molten lava.

On our way through the cafeteria, I catch a glimpse of Ryan at his usual table. He's looking right at you, an evil smirk on his face.

"Stupid troll," I mutter on our way out of the cafeteria. We start down the wide hall, toward your locker. "We *really* need to figure out a way to get him back."

Too bad we still don't have any ideas. You had all night to come up with a revenge plot. Instead, you put all your energy into drawing.

Luckily, we have a master spy on our side.

When you swing open your locker door, a strand of toilet paper comes falling out.

51.

You snap the toilet paper off the floor and race to the boys' bathroom.

Normally, I'd wait in the hall until you're done with whatever it is you do in there. But this time, I follow you inside. We shove our way into the first open stall and lock the door.

I stand on my tiptoes, trying to get a better look at the toilet paper. "What's it say? Is it a good idea? Do you think it'll work? What if—"

FLUSH!

The sound of rushing water is a reminder that we're not alone. And some people might find it a little weird if you started talking to yourself in the boys' bathroom.

Fine then. I'll keep my questions to myself.

While I stand squished in the corner, you slowly read what Anni wrote. From this angle, I can barely see the toilet paper. I only manage to glimpse a few words.

CREATE A DISTRACTION

Once you're done, you crumple the message into a ball and drop it into the toilet.

"Wait, I didn't get to see the whole—"

Once again, I'm interrupted by a flush.

Anni's message spins around and around.

And then it's swallowed by the toilet.

"Thanks a lot," I grumble.

But my disappointment doesn't last long. There's too much to be excited about. Sneaking around! A secret message! Plotting revenge!

It's like we're in a spy movie!

Although—I can't remember any spy movies that take place in the boys' bathroom of a middle school.

You rip off a fresh sheet of toilet paper and begin scribbling on it with a marker. This time, I catch a glimpse of what you've written.

GOT YOUR MESSAGE
THE PLAN IS ON

52.

We stop at Anni's locker on the way to first period. You wait until nobody else is around before slipping the scrap of toilet paper through a slot in the metal door.

53.

The rest of the day hums with jittery energy. Your knee bounces restlessly under your desk during class. You drift through one period after another with a dazed, distracted look on your face. Your attention has been hijacked by the revenge plot. Will it work? Is there anything you've forgotten? Will you get caught?

Being a spy is harder than it looks.

You have enough on your mind already, so I do my best to stay out of your way. During class, I perch myself on a shelf at the back of the room and watch the lesson. When I think I know the answer to the teacher's question, I mumble it to myself, quietly enough that I won't distract you.

If I get the answer right, a happy buzz vibrates through my fur.

And if I get it wrong…

Well, at least nobody hears me.

This works well enough until sixth period Chemistry.

Your teacher, Mr. Gold, has one of those slow, dry voices that can put an entire classroom to sleep. He's droning on about covalent bonds.

When I can't listen any longer, I hop off my shelf and stand under one of the AC vents. Curling myself into a ball, I wait until I hear the sound. A gulp of air somewhere deep inside the ceiling. Followed by a rush of cool wind through the vent.

FWOOSH!

The breeze ruffles my fur and sends me bouncing around the classroom. It's so much more fun than Mr. Gold and his covalent bonds. I drift around the back of class, pinballing between cubbies and bookshelves.

My mind is drifting too.
Deeper and deeper into memory.

54.

This is what I remember:

I'm back in your house—your old house—and there are flowers everywhere. On the dining room table, on the mantel, crowded into the corner. Flowers in every room, bursting out of vases, their petals slowly gathering on the floor and getting squished under people's feet.

All the flowers come with a card attached. And all the cards have the same words written on them.

SORRY FOR YOUR LOSS

In a few days, the flowers will wilt and die. They will hit their expiration date too.

A door rises up in my memory. We're sitting on the floor of your bedroom—your old bedroom—and someone is knocking at the door.

"Hey, Zach?" Ryan's voice echoes in the memory. "Can I come in?"

"No," you say.

"How come?"

"We want to be alone."

"Who's *we?*"

Your eyes dart in my direction. "Nobody."

"Look, we don't have to talk about … *you know.*"

You wince at those words. *You know.* Because of course you know. When he says *you know,* what he really means is *your dad.* It doesn't matter whether you're talking about him—or *not* talking about him—the pain is always there.

Or *almost* always.

There *is* one place you can go. A kingdom of castles and magic, dragons and fairies. You used to take Ryan there BEFORE.

But not anymore.

The whole point is to get *away* from the real world.

As far away as possible.

But Ryan is a part of the real world.

Which means we need to get away from *Ryan.*

He's still trying to talk to you through the door, but we barely hear him. Your attention is on the floor.

A vine has just cracked through the floorboards.

And another.

Soon the vines are everywhere. Growing at a remarkable speed. Climbing the walls like snakes. They twist and twirl over the windows. They wrap themselves across the door. Before long, they've covered every surface, making it impossible for any part of the real world to get inside.

Including Ryan.

The vines muffle his voice. Until—eventually—you can't hear him at all. You like it better this way. Now it's just you and me in a world of magic.

Far away from all the awfulness of the real world.

And far away from Ryan.

55.

No more bouncing for me.

I uncurl my arms and legs and stalk back to my shelf. According to the clock on the wall, there are still twenty minutes left in class. Twenty more minutes of covalent bonds. I'm still not listening though. My thoughts are somewhere else.

I'd forgotten about that day. The two of us on one side of the door.

Ryan on the other.

Vines slowly swallowing more and more of your room.

It was such a long time ago. And such an awful time. Maybe I blocked those memories from my mind.

I wonder if you did the same.

These thoughts follow me for the rest of the school day. Once the final bell rings, we set off in the direction of detention.

Along the way, I glance up at you. "Hey, Zach, maybe you shouldn't go through with this whole revenge plot."

"What're you talking about?" you whisper. "Why would we back out now?"

The trace of a memory in the back of my mind.

Two boys.

And a door standing between them like a wall.

I shake away the memory. "I'm just saying, the situation with Ryan...maybe it's more complicated."

56.

By the time we get to detention, Anni and Ryan are already there. You take your usual seat between them.

"What's up, loser?" Ryan says.

You just smile. "Nice to see you too."

Ryan's face crinkles with confusion. "What're *you* so cheerful about?"

You don't say anything. But your smile only grows.

Grumbling to himself, Ryan opens a folder and yanks out an assignment. Anni is already busy reading her history book. You bury your nose in a book of your own.

And then.

Nothing happens.

Time slowly lurches forward. Pacing across the room, I start to wonder whether you're ever going to go through with this. Maybe something changed. Maybe you've given up the whole revenge plot.

And maybe that wouldn't be such a bad thing.

After you lost your dad, Ryan tried—really, *really* tried— to be there for you. And you blocked him out. That might've been a long time ago. *Years* ago. But the memory is still fresh in my head.

Ryan was your best friend. He cared about you. No matter how things have turned out since, he deserves some kind of credit for that. And I'm seriously starting to think he *doesn't* deserve this revenge plot.

Whatever it might be.

With five minutes left in detention, you snap your book closed.

Shifting in your seat, you turn your attention to Ryan.

Without looking up from his homework, he says, "What're you staring at, loser?"

You cross your arms, leaning back in your chair. "I was just wondering... What's the deal with those Matt guys?"

"I have no idea what you're talking about?"

"I mean, do you actually *like* hanging out with them? Because they seem kind of like huge morons."

This pulls Ryan away from his homework. He sets down his pen and tilts a snide glance in your direction. "Yeah, well, at least they don't spend all their time playing pretend."

The comment is like jabbing you with a needle. I see the pain flash in your eyes.

But only for a split second. Then the smile returns to your face.

"You used to *like* playing pretend," you say. "Remember?"

Ryan snorts. "Yeah, when I was, like, five."

"Oh, so now you're too cool? That what you're saying?"

"I'm *saying*, people grow up. They ditch their imaginary friends and start living in the real world." Ryan narrows his eyes at you. "At least—*most* people."

Another jab. You wince again.

Watching this conversation, my gaze bounces back and forth between you and Ryan. What're you doing? Why are you bringing all this up?

Then I remember. This morning, the boys' bathroom. I couldn't read everything Anni had written on the toilet paper. I only saw a few words.

Create a distraction.

Is that what you're doing? Creating a distraction? If so, it seems to be working. Ryan scoots closer in his chair, speaking in a sharp whisper.

"So, do you and your imaginary buddy still go to that, like, fairy-tale world together?" He lets out a mocking chuckle. "Dude that was, like, your number one hangout spot. Still is, I bet. Pathetic."

Your jaw clenches. You squirm in your seat. If you could, you'd escape from this conversation. Imagine it into oblivion. Do the same to Ryan. Turn him into a troll and send him flailing off the highest peak in the kingdom.

But if you back out now, what will happen to the plan? If you really want to create a distraction, you'll have to keep Ryan's interest. Even if that means sticking with this incredibly uncomfortable conversation.

KLUMP! A strange sound comes from under the table.

Ryan's expression twists with confusion. He starts to turn in his chair. Your eyes fill with panic. And you blurt out, "I still have an imaginary friend!"

Ryan freezes.

He slowly turns his attention back to you. "What did you say?"

You speak up quickly. "That's what you and the Matts keep asking me about, right? If I still hang out with my imaginary friend. Well, it's true, okay? Me and my imaginary friend hang out all the time."

I can't believe you just said all that. To *Ryan.* But I know the reason: You needed to keep him distracted. And it's definitely worked. He sits up a little straighter in his chair. His eyes are on you and only you.

He's forgotten all about the strange noise under the table.

"At least you're finally admitting it," he says. "Is your imaginary friend here now?"

You hesitate.

A moment goes by.

"Well?" Ryan raises an eyebrow. "*Is* he?"

"Y-Yes." A nervous hitch snags your voice. "H-He's here."

"Where?"

You take a deep breath. Turn in your chair. And look in my direction. "He's ... he's over there."

Ryan turns to look. "Where?"

You point. "There."

And all of a sudden...

Ryan's looking at me too. Or—*almost*. His eyes have landed on a spot to my right. The smirking smugness has vanished from his face. He's so genuinely shocked that you're actually telling him about me, he seems to have forgotten—he was in the middle of bullying you.

"So then..." he begins. "What's he doing right now?"

You shrug. "Just standing there."

Ryan continues staring at the spot of the floor that isn't me. "Tell him to say something."

You raise an eyebrow, still looking at me. "Anything you want to say, Shovel?"

Now it's my turn to squirm with awkward silence. I'm not used to having an audience.

You give me an assuring nod. "Go ahead."

"Um..." I clear my throat. "Tell him I said 'Thanks.'"

You just stare. This obviously wasn't what you were expecting. "For what?"

"After what happened to your dad, Ryan came over to your house. A bunch of times, actually. We basically ignored him, but he kept coming anyway. He wanted to be there for you."

Vines climb the walls of my memory.

Filling your room, blocking out the real world.

I blink and the memory is gone.

"I know things have been rough between you guys," I say. "But I just wanted to let Ryan know—I appreciate what he did back then."

A moment passes. Your eyes hang on me.

"Well?" Ryan crosses his arms. "What'd your imaginary friend say?"

His voice pulls your attention away from me.

You look at Ryan closely, like you're searching his features for some trace of the kid he used to be, the kid who sat outside your door, day after day, even though you never let him in.

But before you get a chance to pass along my message, Coach Markey's voice shatters the silence.

"All right, detention's over." He claps a couple of times, as if he's yelling at a basketball team during halftime. "Everybody out!"

For another second, Ryan stares at the spot on the floor that isn't me. I get the feeling he's trying to decide whether or not to say goodbye.

Then he shrugs and stands up.

But he won't be going very far.

Because he's about to literally walk right into a revenge plot.

57.

Ryan's halfway out of his chair when he pitches over sideways. His legs buckle beneath him, his arms flap like a bird that's forgotten how to fly, and all of a sudden...

He tumbles downward.

And lands flat on his face.

"OOF!" His grunt is muffled by the floor. He scrambles, trying to climb to his feet, but his feet aren't cooperating. When one leg goes somewhere, the other skids awkwardly after it.

He scoots and slides and grunts some more.

The whole thing looks ridiculous and painful.

And it was all part of the plan.

While we were busy distracting Ryan, Anni was deep into a task of her own. As soon as Ryan looked in your direction, she dropped under the table and set to work.

Untying Ryan's shoelaces.

Then tying his shoes together.

While she was down there, Anni accidentally kicked one of the table legs. That's what made the *KLUMP*. Ryan almost turned around to investigate the noise. If he *had*, he would've noticed Anni under the table. And figured out what you two were up to. And the whole secret operation would've collapsed.

But you saved the day at the last possible moment.

By admitting we still hang out.

I know how nerve-wracking that must've been for you, but it worked out. Ryan is still lying flat on the ground. His confusion has turned to suspicion. He looks at his shoes.

Then at you.

Then at Anni.

She's back in her chair, holding a phone just above the table, out of view from Coach Markey.

Realization spreads across Ryan's features.

The whole thing was caught on video.

This must be the final stage of the revenge plot. After tying Ryan's shoes together, Anni climbed out from under the table and began recording.

"Whoa, you okay, Ryan?" You drop to the floor. And before Ryan can react, you untie his shoelaces. Leaning in closer, your voice drops to a whisper. "You tripped over your own feet. That's what you're gonna tell Coach Markey."

"I'm not saying that," he hisses back.

You shrug. "Then I guess Anni's gonna have to share the

video she just took. I'm thinking maybe everyone in school might like to see it."

Coach Markey's voice cuts through. "Nasty fall you took there! You all right?"

Everyone's focus is on Ryan.

"Yeah," he mutters, finally. "I'm fine."

"What happened?" asks the coach.

Ryan climbs to his feet, wiping his knees. His untied shoelaces skitter across the floor.

His glance lands on Anni.

She smiles, giving her phone a little shake.

"Nothing," Ryan grumbles. "I just... tripped over my own feet."

"No wonder," says Coach Markey. "Your shoes are untied."

58.

We wait until we get to the sidewalk before we start celebrating. All three of us jumping up and down, cheering and laughing.

Earlier on, I was having second thoughts about the whole revenge plot. But now, I'm totally swept up in the excitement. You pulled it off!

You give Anni a high five. "Dude, the look on his face back there—"

"Priceless!" she says.

"And you captured it all on video! Nice job!"

"I thought it was over when I accidentally kicked the table, but you totally saved the day!"

You shrug. "I just kept him talking."

"Where'd you get the idea to tell him you have an imaginary friend?"

Your eyes flick in my direction. "Um..."

"What?"

Her question hangs in the air.

I look from you to Anni.

And from Anni to you.

The silence stretches.

Until, finally, you begin to speak. "Anni, I..."

Before you can get the rest of the words out, Ryan comes charging in our direction like a troll on the warpath.

59.

"HEY!" Ryan yells. "That was messed up back there!"

Anni crosses her arms. "Yeah, well, so is releasing a bunch of mice and getting us blamed for it."

"We're even now," you add.

Ryan points at Anni. "I want you to delete that video."

Anni laughs at this idea. "Not a chance."

"What're you gonna do with it?" Ryan asks.

"That depends," Anni says. "We might keep it to ourselves. You know, just something to watch whenever we need a good laugh. Or we could go with Option B."

"What's Option B?"

"We share the video with everyone at school."

Ryan has suddenly gone pale. "You can't do that."

"Oh, sure we can," Anni says casually. "We've already created an anonymous account called 'Epic Ryan Fail.'"

"Catchy name, right?" you say.

Ryan no longer reminds me of a troll. More like a regular scared kid.

"What do you want?" he asks.

"We want a truce," Anni says.

"A truce?"

"An end of the conflict," Anni explains. "You don't mess with us anymore. And we won't mess with you."

"If we keep attacking each other, we'll just get more detention," you continue. "Or worse. We could end up suspended like your buddies."

Ryan grits his teeth. "How long is this truce supposed to last?"

"Forever," you answer.

"Forever?"

Anni nods. "No more comments during school. Or outside school. No more picking on either of us. And that *includes* the Matts. You and your friends leave us alone. For good."

"And if we agree to this truce," Ryan says, "you won't share the video."

All three of us nod.

"How do I know you won't just post the video later?" Ryan asks.

Anni takes a second to ponder this before answering with a question of her own. "Are you into spy stuff?"

Ryan stares at her. Clearly, he's wondering where this is going.

So am I.

"Well, I'm sort of obsessed with spies," she continues. "I watched this one documentary about spying, and it had this long part that was all about something called Mutually Assured Destruction. Also known as MAD."

"Cool story." Ryan's voice is flat and sarcastic. "Is there a *point*?"

Anni ignores the rude tone. "MAD came around after the invention of the atom bomb. Suddenly, different countries started creating nuclear weapons. These weapons were basically a million times more powerful than anything that had ever existed. Now, you'd think, with so many of these bombs out there, countries would be launching them at their enemies all the time, right? But that hasn't happened. Not since World War II. Do you know why?"

Ryan looks like a student who's just been stumped in history class. He shakes his head.

"Because of MAD," Anni explains. "If America launched a nuclear missile at Russia, they'd just launch one back. Or maybe more than one. Next thing you know, *both* countries are wiped out."

Anni clenches her hands together, then sends them flaring outward like an exploding bomb.

"Our situation is the same," she says.

I'm finally starting to understand. This is like the Cold War, but for middle school. Instead of launch codes and nuclear weapons, you're dealing with nasty comments and a video that could go viral.

"If you launch an attack," Anni says, "so will we. And if we start something—"

"I'll hit back."

Anni nods gravely. "Mutually. Assured. Destruction."

60.

The truce becomes official with a three-way fist bump.

You, Anni, and Ryan have agreed: no more pranks, no more bullying, no more mean comments.

And no sharing the video.

Now that we have a deal, Anni's gaze moves back and forth between you and Ryan. "Is it really true—you guys used to be friends?"

I'd thought things were tense when we were talking about nuclear weapons. But that's nothing compared to the chilly silence that falls over the conversation now.

Not that you or Ryan actually *need* to say anything. The awkwardness of the moment tells Anni everything she needs to know.

"You *were* friends!" she says.

"That was a long time ago," Ryan responds defensively.

"Why'd you stop hanging out?" Anni asks.

Ryan jabs a thumb in your direction. "It was his fault."

"*My* fault?" You make a face. "Yeah, right! *You* ditched *me.*"

"Oh, whatever—"

"It's true!" you say. "You got all into sports, remember? It was, like, suddenly you never had any time anymore. You were always busy with practice and games and all your new friends."

"I tried to get you to sign up for those teams too!"

You let out a sarcastic snort. "Oh, because I was *SO* into sports!"

"How would you *know?* You never even *tried!*"

"So that made it okay, huh? Since I didn't feel like playing sports, you could just, like, toss me out, like I was a piece of trash?"

"I *tried* to keep hanging out with you! You were too busy playing make-believe by yourself! Or—sorry. *Not* by yourself! You were always with your imaginary fr—"

"Shut up!"

"*You* shut up!"

At this point, you and Ryan are basically yelling at each other. And I'm worried it's only going to get worse. What if this argument explodes into another fight? Anni's words echo in my mind.

MAD.

Mutually Assured Destruction.

If you and Ryan aren't careful, the bombs are going to start flying.

"HEY!" Anni steps between you and Ryan. "Are you serious right now? We literally *just* agreed to a truce! You can't go *five seconds* without getting into another fight?"

You take a step back. So does Ryan. You both mumble your apologies to the sidewalk.

Anni sighs. "That's better."

You look up at Ryan. "I guess...maybe...you might have a point."

This catches him by surprise. "About what?"

"I mean, there were some times when you wanted to talk, or play, or whatever, and I...I pretty much ignored you."

The memory replays in a dark corner of my brain. We were on one side of a door. Ryan was on the other. As he tried to speak to you, vines snaked through the floorboards and climbed the walls.

"I guess I kind of blocked you out," you say now in a voice that's barely a whisper. "I went into my own little world."

"I understand." Ryan shrugs. "I mean...after what happened to your dad..."

Anni looks at you. "What happened to your dad?"

"He, um..." You swallow. "He..."

You can't bring yourself to finish the sentence. Ryan speaks up instead.

"He passed away," he says quietly.

Anni's hands rise to her mouth. "I'm so sorry. I didn't—"

"It was a long time ago," you say quickly. "I was six when it happened."

"That must've been so …" Anni's voice fades, but the look on her face fills in the silence with plenty of meaning.

So heartbreaking.

So awful.

So unfair.

"Yeah." You nod slowly. "It was."

Ryan steps toward you, pulling one hand out of his pocket. For half a moment, it looks like he's going to rest the hand on your shoulder. Then he changes his mind. The hand goes back into its pocket.

"Hey, I…" His words are just as stiff and uncertain as the gesture. "I'm s-sorry too. About all the stuff that's gone down—you know—these past few days. With the Matts. The stuff they said. That was wrong. I probably should've told them to back off, but…"

Anni squints at Ryan. "Um, you make it sound like you were just tagging along. Like this is all the fault of those Matt guys. From what *I've* seen, you were right there in the middle of it."

"No, yeah." Ryan nods. "You're right. It's not only them. I've been kind of a—"

"Giant jerkface?" Anni guesses.

Ryan almost smiles. "I guess you could say that."

"I get that the whole friend thing didn't work out," Anni says. "But, like, how'd you become *enemies*?"

Anni looks from you to Ryan.

No answer.

She runs a hand through her hair. "Sorry, maybe it's a new kid thing. Has this fight been going on for, like, a long time, or…?"

Ryan shakes his head. "No. It's new."

"So, what happened?"

Ryan thinks about this.

Then he tells a story.

61.

Once upon a time, there were two best friends.

One named Ryan.

One named Zach.

They were next-door neighbors. For a time, it seemed they were never apart.

And then, darkness fell over the land.

AFTER Zach's father died, Ryan tried to be there for his best friend. He went to the funeral and memorial service. He showed up at the house with material from the classes Zach missed. He asked—again and again and again—if Zach wanted to hang out. To toss around the Frisbee or play video games or just lie on the floor and stare at the ceiling.

But Zach didn't want to do any of those things.

He didn't want to see Ryan at all.

And so, Ryan was left on the outside.

Alone.

One day, Ryan woke up and realized they weren't even

neighbors anymore. Without warning, Zach and his mom had packed up their things and moved to a new house.

This was the situation they found themselves in:

Zach had lost his father.

Ryan had lost his best friend.

He decided to give soccer a try. He wasn't great. He wasn't even *good*. But that didn't matter. Being out on the grass, under the bright sun, surrounded by other kids and cheering parents, chasing after the ball—that was enough to take his mind off how alone and abandoned he felt.

He joined other teams. T-ball. Flag football. He met lots of new people. Kids who *wanted* to spend time with him. Who *didn't* block him out of their lives.

It was nice to be a part of something again.

Even if he still missed his best friend.

Ryan tried to get Zach to sign up for one of his teams, but Zach never showed any interest in sports.

Time went by.

Weeks and months and years.

Their friendship faded into nothing.

But by then, Ryan had made some new friends.

And they were both named Matt.

62.

The Matts could be loud and rude and mean, but they were also funny and goofy and great at sports. Other kids looked up to them—or at least, they were too intimated to say anything bad about them.

The Matts sat at the best table in the cafeteria. They got invited to the best birthday parties. They were stars. And when Ryan was with them, he was a star too. People laughed harder at his jokes. Girls smiled at him in a new way. Nerds helped him with his homework.

Things were great.

Mostly.

There were moments when Ryan felt like he didn't fit in with his new friends. When he'd look around at everyone else in the group and realize—

He had all the wrong stuff!

His shoes were the wrong brand. His clothes were the wrong style. Even his *backpack* was wrong.

Over and over again, he'd have to beg his parents to take him to the mall—Now! As soon as possible!—so he could get the *right* stuff. Because if he didn't catch up quickly enough, the Matts would let him know *exactly* what was wrong. And they could be ruthless about it.

"What happened to your hair?" Matt Rogers asked one day at school. He leaned in closer, squinting with disgust. "It looks like a cat climbed up there and died."

Matt Reynolds burst out laughing. So did a few others.

Ryan wanted to hide his face in embarrassment. But he'd spent enough time around the Matts and their crew to know—that would be the *wrong* way to react.

Instead, he joined in the laughter, to show everyone just how *little* the comment bothered him.

"You shouldn't talk," he responded, pointing at Matt's shirt. "Especially with those pit stains you're rocking. Seriously, ever heard of a laundry machine?"

And all of a sudden, nobody was laughing at Ryan anymore. They were laughing at Matt Rogers.

But Matt didn't get embarrassed either. Obviously, he knew the *right* way to react. He held up his arm, as if he was proud of the yellow armpit stain underneath. "Want a sniff?"

That was how things worked with the Matts. If Ryan wanted to stay friends with them, he'd have to play along.

And get a haircut.

Ryan sometimes wondered: Was all this worth it? The new clothes, the new hair, the new *him*. Every once in a while, he'd catch a glimpse of himself in the mirror and barely recognize the guy in the reflection.

Did he really *want* this?

But whenever this question started circling his brain, something would remind him: His new life—his new *self*—was actually pretty nice. Like when Coach bumped him up to starting quarterback. Or when Katie Simms—one of the most popular girls in his grade—put her hand on his sleeve and said, "I *like* your shirt." And that was all it took. The doubts vanished.

Yeah, totally worth it.

Over the summer between fifth and sixth grade, Ryan hung out with the Matts practically every day. They went to football camp together. And basketball camp. He got braces (*Katie Simms said she liked those too*). He was happy. He belonged.

Then came the first day of middle school. That morning, he was walking with the Matts when they noticed someone on the sidewalk up ahead. A kid. By himself. Laughing. Completely cracking up. Even from behind, Ryan knew who he was.

Zach.

Was he listening to something? Some kind of hilarious podcast maybe? That was Ryan's first thought. The most obvious explanation for why Zach was laughing so hard. But as Ryan got closer, he could see that Zach wasn't wearing headphones.

So then, what was so funny?

Ryan took another step in Zach's direction. That's when the laughing stopped.

Zach spun around.

All of a sudden, they were facing each other.

Ryan couldn't remember the last time they'd actually *looked* at each other. For the longest time, Zach had basically treated Ryan like he didn't exist. Eventually, Ryan started doing the same. Ignoring his former friend in the halls, treating him like the stranger he had become.

Ryan said nothing. He was still trying to figure out what Zach had been laughing at. That wasn't the way people were supposed to act. It was *wrong*.

But Ryan and Zach weren't the only ones on the sidewalk. The Matts were there too. It didn't take long for them to start teasing Zach, mocking him with their questions.

Dude, what's so funny?

It sounded like you were joking around with someone. There anyone else here?

But not all the questions were for Zach. Matt Reynolds aimed one straight in Ryan's direction.

Hey, weren't you friends with this guy?

Ryan hesitated. But not because he didn't have anything to say. It was the opposite. His brain was brimming with things he wished he could say.

He wanted to ask Zach what was so hilarious.

And why he ditched him all those years ago.

He wanted to know whether Zach still hung out with an imaginary friend.

But Ryan didn't say any of these things. Instead, he looked from Matt to Zach. And in a voice he barely recognized as his own, Ryan said, "That was a long time ago."

A little later that same morning, Ryan was in the cafeteria with the Matts, waiting for first period to start. Others joined them at their table. A crowd was gathering. Looking around, Ryan couldn't believe this was his life. Not that long ago, all these people would've ignored him. Now they were sitting with him. *They* were trying to impress *him.*

The Matts were talking about "that weird kid" they'd come across this morning. And at some point, Ryan heard himself say, "He used to have an imaginary friend."

He's not sure why he said it. It just sort of...slipped out. But now that it was out there, everyone was looking at him. Smiling, waiting for more.

He couldn't leave them hanging.

He had to give them what they wanted.

So he kept talking. "This was after he was *way* too old to have an imaginary friend. And I'd *still* hear him talking to someone who wasn't there."

"Dude!" Matt Rogers smacked him on the shoulder with the back of his hand. "I bet that's who he was joking around with! His imaginary friend!"

Zach was already *that weird kid.*

Now he'd become *that weird kid with an imaginary friend*.

Whenever they saw Zach, the Matts would ask him about this. Zach ignored them. He tried to avoid them. But that only made him a bigger target.

There were moments when Ryan felt bad for Zach. The poor guy. He was like a minnow being hunted by sharks. A few times, he almost told the Matts to back off.

But if he did that, they'd just want to know *why*.

Why're you sticking up for the weird kid with the imaginary friend?

Is it 'cause you used to be besties?

Is it 'cause you're still besties?

No. He couldn't let that happen. He'd already worked so hard to get here. He'd changed his clothes, his hair, everything. He'd finally found some friends again. A place where he belonged.

So he went along with it. When the Matts messed with Zach, Ryan stood there and let it happen. And when that didn't seem like enough, he joined in.

He did whatever he could to stay a part of the group. To keep belonging.

He'd been abandoned once before.

He didn't want it to happen again.

63.

That's where Ryan's story comes to an end.

Now that he's done, I stare at him. It was easier to hate the guy before I knew so much about him.

"I should've left you alone," he says now. There's a soft scratchiness in his voice. "But I was scared. I panicked and said all that mean stuff about you. And your imaginary friend. And it spiraled. And next thing I knew—"

"You were secretly carrying a bunch of mice into detention?" you say.

Ryan lets out a sad chuckle. "Yeah, I guess so."

Anni turns to Ryan. "Seems kinda messed up that you even *want* to stay friends with the Matts."

Ryan doesn't have an answer. But you do.

"I get it," you say. "Friendship is complicated."

You're looking right at me as you say this.

Ryan grinds his heel into the concrete. "I'm sorry."

"Me too," you say.

Anni watches this scene play out, hands on her hips. "So? Are we cool now?"

Ryan nods. "We're cool."

"Yeah," you say. "Cool."

Does that mean you're back to being friends with Ryan? I don't know. Before that part gets explained, your pocket beeps. You reach inside and pull out your phone.

The screen is filled with texts from your mom.

Howd detention go?

You on your way home yet?

Where are you?

Are you OK???

I can feel your mom's worry pulsing from the screen. If you don't get back to her—*SOON!*—the texts will stop.

And the calls will start.

You look up at Ryan and Anni. "I've gotta go!"

The phone is still clutched in your hands. You're already jogging in the direction of home.

You call out, "See you tomorrow at detention!"

I could be wrong, but it sounds like you're actually looking forward to it.

64.

A blank sheet of paper is lying on the desk in front of you. You stare at it for a few seconds.

Then you start drawing.

This time around, you're not drawing a knight. That becomes clear right away. And you also don't go through nearly as many attempts. Maybe it was all that practice you did yesterday. Only three versions end up crumpled in the wastebasket. When you finish the fourth, you nod to yourself, satisfied with the result.

The spy stares out at you from the page.

A hood is pulled over her head. One hand is reaching into her dark cloak, making me wonder: What's she reaching for in there?

A secret code?

A map?

A roll of toilet paper?

You place the drawing on top of the one from yesterday. The picture of the knight.

Then you start on another. It doesn't take long for me to recognize what you're drawing next. It's a troll. The hulking creature is heaving a battle-ax over his shoulder. His clothes are torn and dirty. But there's something about his face.

It's not just that he looks younger.

He also seems... *nicer*.

It's almost like...

Like he could maybe be your friend.

As long as he doesn't bite off your head first.

You add the drawing to the collection. Three pages. A knight, a spy, and a troll.

I wonder what you'll draw next. Obviously, there's still one character you *haven't* attempted. Someone who's been by the knight's side for years. They've traveled the kingdom together. They've survived battles and shipwrecks, dragons and evil spells. And he's standing right beside you.

In case you need a little inspiration, I strike a heroic pose.

But you don't even look my way.

65.

We take our usual spots at the dining room table. You, me, your mom.

And the empty chair.

Some nights, that chair is all you seem to see. It pulls at your attention like a magnet. But this isn't one of those nights. You're too busy piling your plate with seconds.

"Wow!" Your mom gives you an impressed look. "*Someone's* hungry."

"What can I say?" You shove a huge bite into your mouth. Still chewing, you say, "I'm a growing boy!"

Your mom gives you a scolding look, but she can't hide the smile in her eyes. "What've I told you about talking with your mouth full?"

"Um, I don't remember." You open your mouth, displaying half-chewed food. "Did you say it was *hilarious*?"

"Okay, I *really* didn't need to see that!" your mom says, laughing.

You finish chewing, then say, "This is really good, by the way."

"Oh. Thank you." Your mom sounds surprised that you noticed. Maybe that's because you usually don't. "So, how was your day?"

"It was awesome!"

Now she's even *more* surprised. "Anything in particular make it so awesome?"

"Careful..." I warn, thinking back on the day. The revenge plot. Mutually Assured Destruction. "Maybe don't tell her *everything*."

You think for another second. "I don't know. Some days are just better than others."

"I bet you're glad detention's almost over."

You scoop another bite into your mouth. "Actually, it's not that bad."

"Detention? Is not that bad?"

"Yeah."

Your mom leans over and places a hand on your forehead. "Are you *feeling* okay?"

You pull your head away, laughing. "I'm fine!"

And this time, when you use that word—*fine*—you really seem to mean it.

Your mom looks at you like she's still suspicious, like she can't quite figure you out.

She's not the only one.

66.

The world has gone dark outside and I'm in my imaginary top bunk, listening to the sound of your breathing in the bunk below.

"Hey, Zach."

"Mmm?"

"You still awake?"

"Sort of."

"Remember when we went bungee jumping off the side of the Thousand Year Tree?"

"Yeah?"

"We should do that again sometime."

"Yeah, all right."

"How 'bout tonight?" I can hear the hope in my voice.

But you don't even pause to think about the question. You dismiss it with a single word. "Nah."

Hope turns to desperation. "Come on! It'll be fun!"

"It's late, Shovel. I'm tired."

"Okay. I get it."

I close my eyes, but I can't seem to turn off my brain.

"Zach?" I say.

You let out an annoyed sigh. "What?"

"It feels like we're not talking as much as we used to."

"We're literally talking right now."

"I know. But…"

"What?"

"It's just…I mean, I'm glad things are going better with Anni and Ryan. But I'm also kind of worried."

"What're you worried about?"

I hold up one of my hands.

I can barely see it.

My fingers are a faint blur. When I try to concentrate on the middle of my hand, I see the view beyond. The dark ceiling above me.

Your question echoes in my mind.

What're you worried about?

This is what I'm worried about.

My nearly nonexistent hand.

What if I continue fading?

What if I disappear?

I don't say any of this to you though. I don't say anything at all. In the bottom bunk, the rhythm of your breathing has slowed.

You're asleep.

And I'm awake. In the dark. Staring at a hand that has almost faded away into nothing.

67.

By the time I wake up the next morning, you're already banging around in the kitchen, getting your breakfast ready.

I tumble out of my top bunk. I yawn on my way across the room. And again in the hallway. And another time in the dining room.

I feel exhausted and frail. And I don't *look* so hot either. The fading has only gotten worse since last night. My fur looks ragged and pale.

You, on the other hand ...

You're in a fantastic mood. Between bites of your breakfast, you drum on the table with your fingers. When you're finished, you dump the empty bowl into the sink. You give your mom a hug, then scoop up your backpack and start for the door.

As we walk to school, you don't say a word to me. You're too busy whistling a happy melody.

At least *one* of us is having a good morning.

I can barely keep up with you. My feet are dragging. And I know why.

The more I fade, the weaker I get.

68.

On the way to first period, I spot Anni and Ryan in the hall. Talking to each other. Smiling and laughing. Twenty-four hours ago, this would've been unthinkable. Like flipping on the Nature Channel and seeing a lion braiding a zebra's mane.

But now...?

They look like they've been friends since kindergarten.

We walk up to them, catching their conversation somewhere in the middle.

"Yes it was!"

"No it wasn't!"

"I'm telling you, it was all part of her plan!"

"No way!"

"Hey guys." Your voice brings this debate to a sudden stop. "What're you talking about?"

"Oh, good! Zach's here!" Ryan says without a hint of sarcasm. "He can settle this."

Anni smiles at you. "Do you think there was another reason Principal Carter stuck us in detention together?"

You give her a confused look. "What do you mean?"

"Think about it," Anni says. "We'd just gotten into this big fight, and the first thing she does is throw us into a room together? All sharing one little table? With a detention monitor who barely even notices we exist? No way! She obviously had another reason!"

Ryan is shaking his head. "So, what then? You think she was trying to *trick* us into getting along?"

"Wait, slow down!" You hold up your hands like a crossing guard in a busy intersection. "If detention wasn't about punishment, then what *was* it?"

"I keep thinking back to something she said on that first day of detention." Anni strains to remember. "She said, like, she hoped the next five days would give us time to *work through some things*. Those were Principal Carter's exact words. '*Work through some things.*'"

I nod with recognition. "I remember thinking that was kind of a weird thing to say."

Anni keeps talking. "At the time, I figured she just meant, like, she expected us to each deal with our own personal stuff. But now, I'm sort of wondering... What if she was hoping we'd—you know—work through things *with each other*?"

"Well, if that was Principal Carter's plan, it worked. I don't want to punch Ryan in the face." You give Ryan a nudge with your elbow. "At least, not quite as much as before."

The conversation is interrupted when a girl calls out Ryan's name. When I turn around, I see Katie Simms. She's trailed by a couple of other girls.

My fur bristles as they walk through me.

"There you are!" She tosses her blond hair from one shoulder to the other. "I was looking for you."

Her eyes are on Ryan. *Only* Ryan. As if you and Anni aren't even there. I'm used to being invisible. It's kind of my thing. But it's strange to watch someone treat *you* that way.

"Did you do that Geography assignment," she asks.

Ryan shakes his head. "I was gonna do it at lunch."

"Oh, good!" she squeaks. "I'll sit next to you! We can work on it together!"

Katie has glossy hair and name brands all over her clothes. For the first time, she notices who Ryan had been chatting with before her arrival.

Her eyes scan you and Anni.

"Um...*hi?*" Katie's greeting comes out sounding more like a question.

Anni offers a cheerful hello. You wave.

Katie stares for another second, like you and Anni are some strange unknown species.

Then she turns her attention back to Ryan. "I've gotta get to class."

"Oh," he says. "Okay."

She raises one well-plucked eyebrow. "You coming or what?"

Katie doesn't wait for an answer. She turns, hair whipping, and starts walking.

Ryan hesitates half a second. Then gives you and Anni an apologetic shrug and hurries after her.

You let out an annoyed huff. Although…what did you really expect? That you and Ryan were suddenly back to being BFFs? That a truce and a trip down memory lane would cause him to ditch his popular friends?

Yeah, right.

Anni doesn't seem nearly as irritated. She catches your eye, then gives her hair an exaggerated flip. It's a pretty solid impression.

This gets all three of us laughing.

69.

The good mood trails you for the rest of the day like an annoying little puppy that won't leave you alone.

"It's great that you're happy," I say to you after lunch. "But you should be careful."

I don't expect you to reply. Not with so many people around. But I can't keep quiet any longer. This needs to be said.

"Just remember: You've known Anni for just over a week," I point out. "And Ryan? I mean, come on! Till yesterday, he was picking on you nonstop. Now you're acting like the two of them are your *friends*? Bad idea."

You zip to the side, weaving past a crowd of seventh-graders. I walk right through them.

"All I'm saying is, maybe don't rush into anything," I say.

Just like before, you ignore me. Soon we arrive at your locker. When you fling open the door, a surprise falls out.

A scrap of toilet paper.

There's only one person who could've put it there. Watching the toilet paper flutter to the floor, I wonder if Anni is hatching another secret plan. Maybe things with Ryan aren't as sunny as they seem. Maybe this has all been part of a long revenge plot. You and Anni have been tricking him into thinking you're all getting along. And this toilet paper will spell out the next stage of your mission.

Except there's nothing written on the toilet paper. Only a picture of a smiley face.

Anni wasn't sharing some covert message. She was just saying hello.

"Seems like a waste of toilet paper to me," I mutter.

But when I glance your way, I see that the expression on your face is a whole lot like the picture on the toilet paper.

You're smiling too.

70.

I'm bouncing around the back of class when the final bell rings. My feet settle onto the floor as your classmates prepare to leave. Closing books and folders, zipping backpacks. There's an electric buzz in the air. School is over.

But not for us.

We still have detention. As you make your way to Room 107, you seem pleased by this fact. A goofy grin hangs across your face. You look like you're on your way to a movie you've been waiting all month to see.

But as we near Room 107, the grin fades.

I can hear voices inside the room. Ryan and Anni's voices. They're talking about you.

"Was he being serious yesterday?" Anni asks. "About having an imaginary friend?"

"Totally serious," Ryan says. "His imaginary friend's name is Shovel."

"Like the thing you dig with?"

"Yep. They've been hanging out since we were little kids."

"Huh." It sounds like Anni is weighing this information against everything else she knows about you. "I didn't think people our age still *had* imaginary friends."

"They *don't*. But Zach…" Ryan pauses to think. "Zach's different."

You stumble backward a step, like you've been shoved. That last word hangs in the air around us.

Different.

I've spent enough time around people your age to know: Kids don't want to be different. Not really. Maybe they want to be *interesting* or *unique* or *rebellious*.

But *different*?

Different means looks and whispers. It means gossip and teasing. Which is why it hurts so much to hear Ryan use that word. And it's even worse that Anni doesn't have your back.

Actually, it seems like she *agrees* with him.

"It must've been so hard to lose his dad," she says. "I mean, if something like that happened to me, I might still be hanging out with my imaginary friend too."

"You had an imaginary friend?"

"His name was Roogoo. He was hot pink and had a trumpet for a nose."

Ryan laughs at this. And soon Anni joins in. And even

though they're laughing about Anni's imaginary friend, it also feels like they're laughing about *you*.

Like you're nothing more than a joke to them.

Your face has gone red. You shift from foot to foot, shaking your head with anger and shame. Anni and Ryan must've heard the movement, because the laughter has come to a sudden stop. Anni turns in her chair. And that's when she sees you. Standing in the door. Listening to them all this time.

"Zach…" She chokes on your name.

Ryan looks just as startled to see you. "Dude, hey. We—um…we were just—"

But you don't hear the rest of what they have to say. You're already walking in the other direction.

71.

You kick open the door to the boys' bathroom and storm inside. The door slams shut behind you. I step through it.

"Are you okay?"

As soon as this question leaves my mouth, I feel like an idiot. You just overheard Ryan and Anni laughing about you behind your back.

Of *course* you're not okay.

"Sorry. Dumb question." I hop onto the edge of the sink. "But, you know, I *did* try to warn you."

Another thing I shouldn't have said. Right now, the last thing you need is *I-told-you-so*. I should be supporting you, letting you know I've got your back—not bragging about how *right* I was.

Ugh. Could this be going any worse?

You pace from one side of the bathroom to the other, shaking your head furiously.

I slide down from the sink. Talking isn't working. Luckily, I have other tricks up my sleeve.

Or... *in my stomach.*

I reach into my round, fluffy midsection, searching for something to juggle. Something that'll really wow you. By the time I'm done with the show, you won't even *remember* what Anni and Ryan said about you.

"That's weird." I dig deeper into my fur. "Where *is* everything?"

My stomach is usually crammed with *all kinds* of imaginary objects. So why can't I find any of them?

I mutter to myself, "Could've sworn I had a can of garbanzo beans in here *somewhere.*"

I grasp around for a few more seconds, but all I find is a whole lot of nothing. My stomach's out of stock. And I think I know what's to blame.

This is all because of the fading.

My outsides aren't the only part of me that are dwindling. My insides are too. I don't have as much energy anymore. It's harder to keep up with you. And now *this*?

I can't even juggle.

Not that you seem to notice. This whole time, you haven't looked at me once. Your eyes are on the mirror. You stare at your reflection like it just insulted you.

"Hey, listen," I say. "I just want you to know—I've got your back. No matter what anyone else does, I'll always be there for you."

Finally. This feels like the right thing to say. But you don't seem happy to hear it. You stomp to the other end of the bathroom. And bend down. And peer under the closed stall door. After a second, you repeat this process at the other stall. Crouch close to the floor. Look underneath the door.

It takes another moment before I understand.

You're making sure nobody else is here.

"Um. Yeah..." I begin. "Like I was saying... It really doesn't matter what happens with Anni and Ryan. Because I'm here. I'll always be your friend."

You turn to me, a strange look in your eyes. "That's all you want, isn't it? For us to be friends? My best imaginary buddy, forever and ever and ever."

The words you're speaking all seem nice, but the way you're saying them isn't nice at all. Your voice is weighed down with anger.

And you still have that look in your eyes. Like you're seeing me in a whole new way.

"But I know what you actually want," you say. "What you really, *really* want is for me to be a loser. To have zero friends. Except for you. That way, we can always hang out. Just the two of us."

"What? No." I stagger back. "Zach, I—"

Your words collide with mine. "You're *happy* that Anni and Ryan were saying all that stuff about me. You don't want me to have them as friends. Or anyone else. You want me all to yourself."

I feel like a deflated balloon. Like something that's been kicked into the corner and forgotten.

And worst of all.

I think you might be right.

My memory tumbles back to last night. Lying in my imaginary top bunk, staring at my own faded hand. The fear stirring inside me. Fear that I was losing you. That you would replace me with your new friends.

Your *real* friends.

And then this morning. You were in such a good mood. Whistling all the way to school, your face bright with anticipation. I should've been happy for you, but instead I spent the whole time sulking. Annoyed that you were ignoring me. Angry that you wanted to see Anni and Ryan more than you wanted to spend time with *me*.

Your eyes narrow at me. "You've always been jealous of my friends. It was the same when I was little. Before my dad..." Your angry tone is swallowed by sadness. You look away. "Back when Ryan and I were still neighbors, you hated it when I would hang out with him. Because that meant I wasn't hanging out with *you*."

Another memory. This one's from a long time ago. Way back BEFORE. I'm standing on the shore, alone, watching you and Ryan speed away on an imaginary monster truck with floatie wheels, and all I could think was—

I want Ryan to go away.

"You're right," I admit. "I was jealous. I'm sorry. But we can fix this."

"*We?*" Your angry voice echoes against the tile walls. "Don't talk about '*We.*' This is your fault. You're the reason people make fun of me! And the worst thing is—they're right. I *am* too old for an imaginary friend. I should've said goodbye to you a long time ago!"

Like a knife straight through my furry chest, right into my heart. That's how I feel.

I turn away from you, but my glance lands on the long mirror that's hanging on the wall.

And there you are again.

Your reflection, just as furious.

I know what I have to do.

I have to give you what you want.

My footsteps glide silently across the bathroom. When I reach the door, I keep going. I pass through the door like it's not even there.

I don't stop or look back. I don't wait to see if you'll come running after me.

I continue walking.

Away from you.

Alone.

72.

Somehow, without even meaning to, I end up back at Room 107. Standing in front of the door, I glance up at the sign posted above me.

DETENTION

Since I don't have anywhere else to go, I step inside.

Anni and Zach are still seated at their usual spots around the table. They don't notice as I slide into the chair between them. Their heads keep turning to glance at the door.

"Do you think he's coming back?" Anni asks.

Ryan nods. "Why would he skip detention? That'd just mean *more* detention."

But Anni doesn't look so sure. "It's been, like, five minutes."

"I feel like such an idiot." Ryan slumps lower in his chair. "We shouldn't have been talking about him like that."

"It's my fault. I'm the one who asked about his imaginary friend."

"It's not your fault. I'm the whole reason we're here. I should've left him alone."

If I could join their conversation, I'd say that neither of them are to blame. I'm the one who stuck around long past my expiration date. The one who jealously hoarded our friendship.

This is all my fault.

But I don't bother saying any of this out loud. It wouldn't make any difference. The only one who would hear me is you.

And you're still nowhere to be found.

"I hope he's okay," Anni says.

"Why *wouldn't* he be?" Ryan asks.

Anni shrugs. "He looked pretty upset."

"He probably just needed some time to, like, cool down."

"And then what?" Anni chews her lip. "He's gonna just stroll back into detention? Late? And it's gonna be like none of this ever happened?"

"Maybe," Ryan says hopefully.

Anni shakes her head. "I think we should do something."

"Like what?"

Anni doesn't have an answer to this. All she can do is look back at the door for the thousandth time, as if that will bring you back.

But still.

No sign of you.

"Do you have his number?" Ryan asks.

"No." Anni sighs. "We talked about exchanging numbers but decided it was better to communicate through toilet paper."

"Toilet paper?"

"It was part of our secret plot to get revenge against you."

Ryan stares at Anni like she just sprouted a third eye. "I have so many questions right now."

"What about you?" Anni says. "Don't you have his number?"

Ryan shakes his head.

Anni looks surprised. "I thought you guys used to be best friends."

"Yeah, when we were like *six*," Ryan says. "We didn't have phones yet."

A blanket of silence falls over the conversation. I glance back and forth between Ryan and Anni. Worry is sketched across their faces.

It's strange being in this room without you. It's strange being *anywhere* without you. This isn't how our imaginary friendship is supposed to work. For my entire life, I've been right there by your side.

Now—being away from you—it feels wrong.

I should've never left you alone in that bathroom.

I glance down at my stomach, but all I see is a faint shimmer of fur.

I have to find you before...

Before I've faded away completely.

I leap out of my chair and hurry out of the room. The hallway is empty. Everyone else has left for the day. When I get to the boys' bathroom, I rush through the closed door.

"Zach, I—"

My voice drops into silence.

You're not here.

I check under the stall doors, like you did earlier. Nope. No sign of anyone.

The bathroom is empty.

You're gone.

73.

On my way back to Room 107, I cling to a thin thread of hope. During the time I've been gone, maybe you returned to detention. And the only reason why I didn't see you on my way back to the boys' bathroom is because you took a different route. And now you're sitting at your usual spot, between Anni and Ryan, wondering where I went.

This hopeful vision fizzles away as soon as I step into Room 107. You're not here.

Worry twists inside me. Anni and Ryan look just as nervous. Anni's hands are clasped under the table, her fingers twisted into knots.

"He's not coming back," she says grimly.

Ryan doesn't try to argue with her. "Where do you think he went?" he asks.

"He walks to school, right? I bet he went home." As Anni speaks, I can see something in her eyes. The beginning of an idea. "Do you know where he lives?"

Ryan thinks about this. "I don't know. I mean, after he moved away, I only went to his house a few times. Since he never wanted to see me anymore, I stopped going. That was years ago. I was just a little kid then, and—"

Anni cuts him off. "But you can at least remember what part of town it's in? Right?"

"Yeah. I guess."

"And once you find the street, you'll probably recognize the house?"

Ryan gives her a closer look. "What're you saying? Like, I should go see him?"

Anni shakes her head. "*We* should go see him."

"When?"

She answers right away. "Now."

"Um, in case you forgot, we're stuck in detention." Ryan gestures to the room around them. "We can't go *anywhere* right now."

"It's our fault he's not here. He already thinks we don't care about him. The longer we wait, the worse that's gonna get."

Ryan squirms in his seat.

Anni presses on. "Look, I know you and Zach aren't friends anymore, but you *used* to be. You were *best* friends. That has to mean something. You tried to be there for him back after his dad died. And, yeah, I know. He shut you out. But this is another chance. You can be there for him *right now.*"

"Okay," Ryan says softly.

Anni blinks. "Really?"

He nods. The next time he speaks up, his voice is more forceful. "Let's go."

"All right!" Anni pumps her fist. "So now we just need a way to sneak out. I was thinking we could cause some kind of distraction at the other end of the room. Maybe you could, like, throw something over there. And then—when Coach Markey gets up to investigate—we make our escape. Unless . . ." Anni rubs her chin, thinking. "You don't have any more mice in your backpack, do you? Because if you do—"

"I think maybe you've seen too many spy movies," Ryan interrupts. Then he points at Coach Markey, hunched at his desk, staring at his computer and scratching his backside. "Since when does he pay attention to *anything* we do? If we walk out right now, I doubt he'll even notice."

"But after detention's over . . .?"

"*Then* he'll notice." Ryan shrugs. "But by that point, we'll already be gone."

"You know he's gonna tell Principal Carter, right?" Anni says. "We'll probably get into trouble. *More* trouble."

"I know," Ryan says. But he doesn't look nervous. "It's like you said: I couldn't be there for Zach after what happened to his dad. But maybe I can be there for him now."

A half-smile flicks across Anni's face. "You ready?"

Ryan nods. "Ready."

It's not much of a secret mission. There's no need to

smuggle a boxful of mice or exchange toilet paper messages. Anni and Ryan just stand up and walk out of the room.

The entire time, I keep my eye on Coach Markey.

For a split second, I'm terrified that he's turning to look, that he's about to notice.

False alarm. He's just giving his butt another scratch.

Anni and Ryan quietly slip out of the room.

So do I.

74.

Ryan wasn't kidding when he said he can't remember where you live. He leads Anni and me on a zigzagging path, down one street and up another. We pinball from neighborhood to neighborhood. Whenever we get somewhere new, Ryan looks around, trying to figure out whether we've finally found the right street.

So far, we haven't.

Every time they take a wrong turn, I let out an annoyed groan. I know exactly where we need to go, but there's nothing I can do to tell them.

It's never felt so frustrating to be imaginary.

A couple of times, I jump up and down, pointing in the right direction, hollering at the top of my lungs. "IT'S THIS WAY!"

Not that I expect anyone to hear me. It's just my way of venting.

After twenty minutes of this, Anni gets the idea to use

Google Maps on her phone. Every time we walk down a street, she drops a pin.

"That way, we can at least get an overview." She shows Ryan the screen. Little red pins are dotted all across the map. "Now we know where we've been. And where we still need to go."

Ryan waves away this idea. "I don't need your phone. I'm pretty sure his house is …" Ryan glances left, then right. He points. "That way!"

Anni is already shaking her head. She holds up her phone. The map on the screen shows a cluster of dropped pins. "We've already been down that street."

"Oh." Ryan scratches at his head. "Duh. Of course. I didn't mean *that* street. I meant …"

Another second of hesitation.

Ryan looks around.

Then he nods straight ahead.

"It's probably right up that way."

Anni shakes her head again. "We've been there too."

Ryan looks annoyed. But he just sighs. "Fine. Where does your *map* say we should go?"

Anni and her map lead us south along the edge of Gibbs Park, then west. With each street we walk down, she adds another pin. We still haven't arrived at your street, but we're getting closer. At one point, we even walk past your street. But instead of turning left, we head straight.

Then right.

Then right again.

Anni circles back to your street. She points. "We haven't been there yet. Should we check that street out?"

"YES!" I scream at the top of my lungs.

Ryan isn't nearly as enthusiastic. But he follows Anni anyway. As we walk, I glance around at all the familiar houses and yards and driveways. And up ahead...

Your house.

But will Ryan recognize it?

I come to a stop at your driveway and wait. There are plenty of clues. Your mom's car is parked in the driveway. The same car she was driving when you and Ryan were still best friends. And your last name is printed on the mailbox. It's too far away to see from the street, but if Ryan and Anni get a little closer...

They continue walking.

Past me.

And your house.

"IT'S RIGHT HERE!" I jump up and down, flapping my arms. "YOU JUST HAVE TO—"

Ryan staggers to a halt. His head is tilted. Almost like he heard something. The faint sound of an imaginary furball screaming his lungs out.

"I think..." He starts to turn. His eyes land on your driveway. "I think that's his mom's car."

"Really?" Anni asks.

"YES!" I yell.

"Yes," Ryan says.

Ryan is already crossing the driveway. Sure enough, when he gets to the mailbox, he spots your last name.

"This is it!" he shouts.

Anni and I are both clapping and cheering. The three of us race to the front door, smiling with relief and excitement.

Anni rings the doorbell.

I hear the muffled thump of footsteps somewhere inside.

A second later.

The door swings open.

Your mom looks down at Ryan and Anni. Her expression goes from confusion to recognition to surprise.

"Ryan?" she says.

"Hi, Ms. Belvin." Ryan jabs a heel into the doormat. "It's been a long time."

"It sure has!"

Even after all the trouble Ryan's gotten you into, your mom is all smiles. Her gaze moves to Anni.

"Hello," she says.

"Hi." Anni gives a half-wave. "My name's Anni. Ryan and I are in detention with Zach." She turns to Ryan. "And we're also his friends."

Another flash of surprise in your mom's face. "Well, that's . . . great."

She takes a step back, gesturing into the house.

"Would you like to come in?"

"Actually," Ryan says, "we were hoping to talk to Zach, if that's okay."

A wrinkle forms in your mom's forehead. "Zach's not here."

Silence lands in the middle of the conversation like a bomb. I repeat your mom's words, sure I must've misheard her.

Ryan and Anni are obviously just as stunned.

A question pierces the silence:

If Zach isn't home, then where *is* he?

75.

Your mom tries to reach you.

Again and again and again.

She calls, but you don't answer.

She leaves voice mail messages, but you don't call back.

She texts, but you don't reply.

Pacing the living room, she clutches her phone. I've never seen her so worried.

"Did he say anything?" she asks. "Anything about where he was going?"

Anni and Ryan shake their heads.

So do I.

"Should we check his room?" Anni asks. "You know, maybe he left something in there that'll tell us where he went."

Footsteps clatter across the living room and down the hall. As soon as we get to your room, everyone starts looking around. We're like the weirdest team of detectives—

two kids, one mom, and one imaginary friend—searching for clues.

It's hard to find much of anything in such a mess, though. Opening the closet just causes laundry to spill out. The floor is littered with empty soda cans and plastic wrappers. The wastebasket is overflowing with crumpled paper.

Ryan notices your desk. Three pages, a drawing on each. "Did *Zach* draw these?"

Your mom smiles at the pictures. "He's been drawing a lot over the last couple of days. Said it was something Principal Carter suggested he should try."

Anni's eyes move from the knight to the spy to the troll. "These are seriously amazing!"

Ryan picks up one of the pages. The picture of the knight. "Hey, uh, does this guy look sort of … familiar?"

Your mom's face lights up with recognition. "It's Zach."

"Oh my gosh, it *is*!" Anni says. "That's totally Zach!"

Your mom points to another drawing. The spy. A hand reaching under a cloak. A face peering out from under a hood.

"I think this one's you," she says to Anni.

"Really?" Anni takes a closer look. "Oh, yeah! I guess I see what you mean!"

Ryan eyes the picture of the troll. "But then, who's *this* one supposed to be?"

Anni looks from the troll to Ryan.

From Ryan to the troll.

And she lets out a snort of laughter.

Ryan's eyebrows sink. "What's so funny?"

"Don't you see it?" Anni asks.

"See *what*?"

She points to the page. A brutish troll, heaving an axe over his broad shoulders. "Ryan, this is *you*."

Ryan shakes his head. "No way! That doesn't look anything *like* me!"

"It's *a hundred percent* you!" She holds up the page for your mom. "Right, Ms. Belvin?"

But your mom isn't listening to the debate. Her attention is on something else.

Your backpack.

It's lying on the floor beside the closet. She crouches down and unzips the front flap. Inside are books and folders.

And a single scrap of toilet paper.

With a drawing of a smiley face on it.

Your mom holds up the toilet paper. "What do you think *this* is?"

"I drew that," Anni says. "I put it in his locker earlier today."

Your mom looks confused. "You put toilet paper in Zach's locker?"

"It's sort of an inside joke," Anni replies.

Your mom accepts this with a shrug. Her glance travels from Anni to Ryan. "You see what this means, right?"

"That Anni has a really weird sense of humor?" Ryan guesses.

"It *means* Zach came back here after school. He dropped off his backpack in his room. He must've left again before I got home."

We inspect the rest of the house (*no sign of you*) and look in the backyard (*ditto*) before ending up in the garage. That's where we find the next big clue.

Your bike is gone.

"Wherever Zach went next—it must be kind of far away," Ryan says. "Why else would he go by bike?"

I scan the rest of the garage. Unlike the messy chaos of your room, everything here is neatly organized. Cardboard boxes are labeled and stacked on shelves. Tools hang from a pegboard in even rows. There are even outlines to show exactly which tool goes in which spot.

The group is standing close by, discussing where you went on your bike. But I barely hear them. I'm too busy staring up at the board. All the tools are there, hanging where they're supposed to be.

Except for *one*.

I can tell by the outline which one it is. The shape couldn't be more obvious. Looking at it now, understanding burns bright in my mind.

I know exactly where you went.

In the next moment, I'm on the move. Racing past the others and through the closed garage door.

On my way to find you.

76.

All along, the key to finding you was right there ...

In my name.

It was the thing you used to dig a hole to the other side of the earth. And to bury a box of reminders in the backyard.

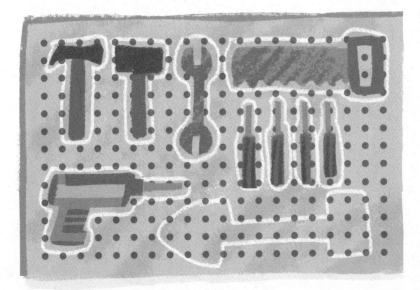

It was the only tool that was missing from the pegboard in your garage.

A shovel.

There in the garage, I traced the outline of the missing tool. This time, it wasn't a plastic toy. It was your mom's hand shovel, the one she uses in the garden.

I'm pretty sure I know what you need it for.

You're going back to your old house.

You're going to dig up the box.

77.

I run as fast as I can. All the way to the front yard. That's how far I get before I stagger to a stop, wheezing and coughing and completely exhausted.

I'm gasping for air. My legs feel like Jell-O.

Hunching over, I place my hands on my knees. Except—I can barely *see* my hands. Or my knees. They've faded into nearly nothing. And so has my energy.

I'm struggling to make it out of your yard. How will I ever get all the way to your old house?

I glance back at your front door, wishing for the others to come bursting through. Your mom, keys in her hand. Everyone piling into the car. Including me. I could hitch a ride across town and we'd be there in a few minutes.

But they don't know about the box. They weren't there when you buried it in the backyard of your old house. Even if they *did* notice the missing shovel, they'd never guess where you were taking it. And there's no way for me to tell them.

Meanwhile, you're still out there. Alone. Whether you know it or not, you need a friend.

Even an *imaginary* one.

I start running again, as fast as my weak legs can carry me. But when I get to the street, I collapse into a heap of faded fur.

I can't do this.

I've dwindled away too much.

Letting out another moan, I flop over onto my back. Far above me, a fluffy white cloud drifts lazily across the sky. As I watch it, an idea begins to take shape in my head.

Maybe…

Possibly…

I climb back to my feet. All of a sudden, I notice things I hadn't noticed before. The wind rustling through my fur. Leaves shivering in the breeze.

I squeeze my arms tight against my puffy stomach. And fold up my legs. Just like I've done a million times before. Whenever things get boring, I'll curl up next to the nearest AC vent and wait for the sound. A sudden gulp of air. As if the building is holding in a burp.

Except this time, it's not the air conditioner I'm waiting for.

It's another gust of wind.

I'm ready when the next gust blows past. *WHOOSH!* It rushes through my fur and pushes me down the street like a balloon in the breeze.

Carrying me closer to you.

78.

Good thing the wind's blowing in the right direction. It bounces me across lawns and over driveways, through intersections and between houses. Whenever I veer off course, I uncurl myself and walk to where I need to go. Once I'm in a better position, I squeeze myself into a ball again and wait for the next breeze.

Bounce, bounce, bounce.

It's been years since the last time I saw your old house, but I still remember exactly where it's located. As I drift in that direction, I find myself thinking about the Butterfly Effect, the Elephant Fart Effect, the *whatever you want to call it.*

If you'd gotten to detention just a minute earlier, or little bit later, you might not have overheard Anni and Ryan talking about you.

Which means all the stuff that came afterward...never would've happened.

Our fight in the boys' bathroom.

Anni and Ryan's escape from detention.

The search for your house and the meeting with your mom.

All erased. Gone. *Poof.*

You would still be friends with Anni and Ryan. And I would still be right there by your side.

Instead, I'm worried sick, bouncing like a purple tumbleweed toward your old house.

I just hope I'll find you there.

79.

I bounce to a stop in front of your old house. It's been so many years since I've seen the place. Everything is smudged with memories. There's the tire swing your dad used to push you on. And the street where you learned to ride a bike. And the front steps where your parents would sit, watching you play in the grass.

A lot of memories. But no sign of you. Or anyone else. The driveway is carless. The windows are dark. There's nobody in the tire swing.

But when I make my way around the side of the house, I spot your bike lying in the grass beside a wooden fence.

I walk past your bike, through the fence, and into the backyard.

The backyard looks smaller than I remember. The grass is scattered with toys and playthings. A pink tricycle. A rubber ball. A little kid must live here.

I hurry across the yard, stopping once to catch my breath.

In a corner of the yard, I notice a movement behind a row of bushes. You. Hunched close to the ground, digging with the hand shovel.

As I get closer, I see that the ground all around you is scarred with holes and chunks of dirt. You've already tried digging up a dozen spots.

And you still haven't found the box.

I call out, "ZACH!"

You turn around. You don't look happy to see me. "I told you—I don't want to be your friend anymore."

Another crack in my broken heart.

I take a step toward you. "This isn't your house anymore. You could get into big trouble for sneaking in."

"There's nobody home. They won't even know I was here."

I scan the ravaged ground around you. Little craters everywhere. "You sure about that?"

"I'll fill in the holes," you say. But instead, you do the opposite. You start digging another one.

"Zach, your mom's worried about you," I say. "She keeps trying to call and text."

"Phone's battery died," you say blankly. "I want to be alone anyway."

You plunge the shovel's blade into the ground again. But all you uncover is more dirt. The box isn't down there. Just like it wasn't at the bottom of any of the other twelve holes.

"I don't get it," I say. "Why *now*?"

You glance up at me. "What do you mean?"

"The box has been buried for *years*. If you wanted to get it back so badly, you could've come back anytime. So why now?"

You stab the shovel into the ground again and again and again. Your words come between crunches of the blade.

"The whole reason I buried my dad's old stuff was because it made me sad." *CRUNCH!* "Like, if I didn't see it, I wouldn't feel bad anymore." *CRUNCH!* "Except burying it didn't fix anything." *CRUNCH!* "I was still sad." *CRUNCH!* "All the time." *CRUNCH!* "But when I was in Principal Carter's office, she said this thing." *CRUNCH!* "When you try to avoid something, you actually make it bigger." *CRUNCH!* "That got me thinking." *CRUNCH!* "That's what I was doing with the box." *CRUNCH!* "Taking all the stuff that makes me sad and hiding it underground." *CRUNCH!* "But that won't get rid of the sadness." *CRUNCH!* "It only makes it bigger."

The digging stops.

So does the talking.

Without the sound of your voice or the slice of the shovel, the backyard suddenly seems very quiet.

My words fill the silence. "If you find the box, do you think you'll feel better?"

You shrug. "Maybe. Maybe not. But this is what I need to do. I can't keep pretending the bad stuff isn't there."

Pretending. The word sticks in my mind like a splinter.

You have other ways of playing pretend. I should know. I'm one of them.

For now, at least.

I'm fading fast. But this isn't a pity party. At least I'm here with you now. Still. After all these years. I may not know how much time I have left, but I *do* know this: As long as I'm your friend, I might as well help.

I turn my attention to the cratered ground. Concentrating. Trying to remember that day. The last time we were here in this part of the backyard. Where were we standing? What was around us?

I take a step away from where you've done most of the digging. When I stare at the patch of grass, my fur buzzes. There's something familiar about this spot.

"Try over here!" I say.

You hunch down and start digging. With each crunch of the shovel, my certainty grows. This is it! Has to be!

The hole grows.

Deeper.

Deeper.

Deeper.

Except all you find is more dirt. I can see how upset it's making you. You're not even really digging anymore. It's more like you're hitting the ground with the shovel, taking out your anger. Dirt and grass fly everywhere.

This isn't just about the box. I can see it in your eyes. This is also about the stuff you overheard Anni and Ryan saying earlier. Or maybe it goes back farther. *Years.* All the way back to the moment your dad got sick. All the sadness, the unfairness, the disappointment, ripping through you like a storm.

The shovel rises and falls. The blade smacks the earth again and again and—

CLUNK!

A new sound echoes in my ears. The sound of metal hitting plastic.

You drop the shovel. Both of us lean forward, peering into the hole.

Poking up from the bottom of the hole, half-buried in dirt, is a tiny plastic troll.

80.

Five years.

That's how long this box has been buried.

So much has happened since it went into the ground. We changed houses. You lost friends and gained friends. I started fading again.

And now.

After all this time.

Here we are again.

You reach into the hole and pull out the object on top. The troll. Its gray face is crusted with dirt. There's a diagonal cut across the monster's chest where you hit it with the shovel.

It's not the first time you attacked a troll.

The troll slides into your pocket. After a little more digging, you manage to lift the box out of the ground.

I cast a nervous glance back at the house. It used to be our house. Now it belongs to someone else, and they could get home any second.

"We should probably go," I say.

But you aren't listening. All your attention is on the box. On the things inside. Things that belonged to *him*.

You let out a trembling breath. A tear traces down your cheek. With a sniff, you wipe it away, leaving a smudge of dirt behind.

Then you drop the shovel into the box. Bending down, you wrap your arms around the plastic sides and lift.

Halfway across the yard, I glance back. "Zach, you..."

Forgot to fill in the holes. That's what I was about to say. But I stop myself. Going back now would just mean more time in this backyard. More danger of getting in trouble for trespassing on someone else's property.

Anyway, the holes are mostly hidden. Off in the corner, behind a row of bushes. I doubt anyone will even notice. And if they *do*, they'll just think their yard was invaded by a deranged hedgehog.

So I don't say anything. And you don't go back. We make our way across the yard, the box rattling with each step you take.

At the wooden fence, we come to a stop. You lean over and drop the box on the other side.

"Uh, Zach?" I point to the gate door a few feet away. "Can't you just go through that way?"

You shake your head. "Already tried that when I got here. It's locked. Had to climb it."

And you're going to have to climb it again. Luckily, the

fence is only about half your height. You boost yourself up, then swing a leg around. For a single wobbly moment, you're halfway over, flat on your stomach.

That's when I see it.

A loose sliver of wood, poking out of the fence like a spike.

"Zach, watch out for the—"

Before I can say anything else, your arm slides over the sharp piece.

"Argh!"

Your pained voice. And the sight of blood. *Your* blood. On *your* arm. It hits me all in a flash.

Then you flop over the fence and land on the other side.

81.

There's no need for me to climb the fence. I can step through it.

I arrive on the other side an instant later. You're leaning against the fence, gripping your arm. Blood spills through your fingers.

"Zach!" My voice strains with worry. "You've gotta get help."

"It's just a scratch," you insist.

You start to walk. But after two steps, you stagger against the house.

"Okay, maybe more than a scratch," you admit.

I hurry to your side. "You sure your phone's dead?"

Still gripping your injured arm, you pull the phone out of your pocket and press a button.

Nothing. The screen stays dark.

"Dead," you mutter, sliding it back into your pocket.

I feel so useless. I can't put my arms around you. They

would pass right through you. I can't scream for help. Nobody would hear me.

Let's face it. I'm nothing but an imaginary furball that exists inside your head.

But as long as I'm inside your head, I can still help.

"You're all right." I force my voice to keep steady. "Let's just keep moving. One foot in front of the other."

Whenever we're off on our fantastical adventures—scaling perilous mountains or fighting armies of trolls—the knight is in charge. He's protected by his armor and his magic sword. It's the furball who usually needs the motivational speeches.

Now the roles are reversed.

"We're gonna get through this," I say in my most heroic voice. "Just keep pressure on your arm. And don't even *think* about looking at it, hear me? You know what the sight of blood does to you. We don't need you passing out on us."

This is no exaggeration. Even a *glimpse* of blood is enough to make you woozy. If you got a good look at the cut on your arm, it could make you faint. I've seen it happen before. I don't want to see it happen again.

"What're we supposed to do now?" you ask, then look back at your bike. It's still lying in the grass. The box is next to it. "I can't ride a bike like this. And there's no way I'll be able to walk all the way home."

"We don't have to go home," I say. "We just have to go next door."

Your eyes light up. "Ryan's house."

After we moved out, Ryan stayed put. And his mom's car is parked in the driveway.

When you knock—sure enough—she answers. After all these years, I wonder if she'll recognize you. Turns out there's no need to worry. The second she sees you on her doorstep, she says, "Zach!"

Then she sees your arm. The blood dripping through your fingers, staining your shirt.

Her eyes go wide. "What happened?"

"I scratched my arm. I don't think it's bad." You lift your arm, showing her the cut. "Just a little bl—"

Uh-oh. You just caught sight of the injury. That's all it takes. The color drains from your face. You reach out a hand, trying to steady yourself, but there's nothing to hold on to. Just empty air. And me.

You tilt sideways. The leaning tower of Zach.

Then gravity pulls you the rest of the way down.

Ryan's mom calls out with alarm. "ZACH!"

But by then, you've already fainted.

82.

I can't tell you what happened next. Right around the time you fainted...

I fainted too.

I was already so weak. I'd faded away to nearly nothing. And then—seeing your bloody arm, watching you crumple on the doorstep of Ryan's house—

It was just too much.

A moment after you dropped, my vision blurred and my legs gave up on me.

The world went dark before I hit the ground.

83.

When I open my eyes again, there's a crowd outside Ryan's front door. His mom is here. And so is yours. Ryan and Anni are here too. They're all gathered around, peering down at the same thing.

You.

It looks like you just woke up. There's a bandage wrapped around your injured arm. Voices bounce back and forth around us, everyone trading off. Making sure you're okay, catching you up on everything you've missed.

The escape from detention.

The search for your house.

The inspection of your artwork.

While you were out cold, Ryan's mom bandaged your arm. Then she called your mom. She was surprised to learn that Ryan was at your house already.

Everyone got here a few minutes after that.

Anni and Ryan run to fetch your bike and the box from

the house next door. Which used to be *our* house. When your mom gets her first glimpse of the items *inside* the box, she nearly faints too.

"Those are your dad's old things!" she says. Her tone is a mixture of disbelief and amazement. "Where'd they come from? And what happened to your arm?"

Sitting on the doorstep, you tell them everything. A story that starts when you were six, roaming around your old house, searching for sad reminders of your dad. Flash forward five years and you're skipping detention to journey across town, on a mission to dig up the box that had been in the ground all this time.

Hearing you describe it now, the whole thing sounds like something you would've dreamed up in your imagination. A hunt for buried treasure. It even has a bloody ending.

Your mom peers at the box. Her eyes slowly move from one item to another. A pair of sunglasses. A plastic dragon. Headphones. They look ordinary, but they're so much more.

They were *his*.

"All this time, I thought they were lost." She sniffs, wiping away a tear.

You bring a hand down on her shoulder. "I'm sorry. I should've said something. I just—"

"It's alright." She smiles. "We all have our ways of dealing. And you were so young."

"Do you feel any better now?" Anni asks. "I mean, now that you got the box back?"

You think about this for a second. "Well, my arm still hurts. Like, a lot. And I'm probably gonna get in even more trouble at school once Principal Carter finds out I ditched detention. But…yeah." You let out a chuckle of surprise. "Actually, I *do* sort of feel better."

"Are you sure you didn't hit your head when you fainted?" Ryan asks.

Anni jabs him with her elbow.

You laugh again, harder this time. "I think I'm okay. Or, at least, I'm gonna be."

This brings a smile to my face.

I think you might be right.

84.

The moms are talking inside. The rest of us are out on the lawn. The sun just dipped below the trees.

"I'm so sorry," Anni says.

Ryan nods. "Yeah, we shouldn't have been talking about you like that."

But you're not upset anymore. "Guys, it's okay. I mean, I know it's weird. Most kids my age don't have imaginary friends. Trust me, I never would've expected to still be hanging out with a gigantic invisible furball."

Your eyes land on me. There's a sad smile on your face.

You continue. "It's just…after my dad…the real world didn't make sense anymore. But when I was inside my own head—just me and Shovel, playing pretend…*there* I had control. I made the rules. I was the hero. Like, literally a knight in shining armor."

You let out a long breath.

"I liked the feeling." You shrug. "I didn't want to give it up."

"We all play pretend," Anni says. "In our own ways. Like, in my head, my life's basically one big secret spy mission. And Ryan likes to imagine he's one of the cool kids when, obviously, he's a weirdo like us."

"Hey!" Ryan snatches a twig off the lawn and throws it at Anni.

"But seriously," Anni continues. "Everyone has their way of dealing with stuff. And if you ever wanna talk to someone who *isn't* a giant furball, we're around."

"Can I tell you guys something?" Ryan looks both ways, like he's making sure nobody else is around to overhear what he's about to say. "This might sound crazy, but I'm gonna miss detention."

"I *told* you!" Anni points at Ryan. "Total weirdo!"

Another twig goes flying in her direction.

"I'm gonna miss it too," you admit. "I mean, I'd be cool with never watching Coach Markey scratch his butt again. Like, *ever*. But the rest of it wasn't so bad."

"I guess after Principal Carter finds out what we did, we'll end up with more detention," Anni says. "So at least there's that."

The conversation is put on pause. A car just pulled into the driveway next door. Our old house. A family gets out of the car. Two dads and a little girl with curly brown hair. She looks about the same age you were when we first met.

I think of the toys and playthings I glimpsed in the backyard of the old house. A pink tricycle. A rubber ball. A splash pool. They belong to her.

The girl flops onto the tire swing, stomach-first. "Somebody push me!"

"Not now, button," one of the dads says.

"Pleeeaaaase!"

Her dad sighs. "Five minutes. Then it's time for dinner."

"Yeaaah!"

The dad sends his daughter spinning and squealing on the tire swing. In my memory, a different dad pushes a different kid.

85.

It's later now. The sky's gone dark. Streetlights have blinked on. The little girl is done swinging. She's gone inside with her dads.

Anni's parents arrive to pick her up. Ryan waves to you, then goes inside.

Now it's just you, me, and your mom.

We climb into the car. Us in the back, your mom in the front. Seatbelts click. The engine rumbles.

But the car stays put.

Your mom's eyes drift out the side window, toward our old house. "I haven't seen this place since the move."

"Me neither," you say.

"Same," I add.

"You know, back then I said we had to move because the house was too big," she says. "But that wasn't the reason.

Not really. The truth is … being there was just too hard. Everything there made me think of *him*. And I missed him. So, so much."

Her voice is quiet. Her eyes hang on the house.

"So I came up with an excuse to leave," she continues. "Just to get away. So we could start over somewhere else. Somewhere new."

"The house was like the box," you say.

Your mom's glance flickers to the back seat. "What?"

"Like, how I didn't want to see all his stuff. Because it reminded me of him. And made me sad. So I buried it in the yard. That's sort of what you did with the house. You didn't want to be around the reminders either. But you couldn't bury a whole *house*, so—"

"I moved." She lets out a sound. Something between a laugh and a sob. "I guess we have that in common."

For a few seconds, the only sound in the car is the hum of the engine. Your mom's gaze drifts out the window again, watching the house.

"I let myself hate that house. Because that's where your father died. But…" She exhales a slow breath. "It's also where he *lived*."

You lean forward in the back seat. Your hand comes to rest on her shoulder. "It was a great place to grow up."

"Yeah?"

"Yeah."

She turns in her seat. Her eyes find you. "If your father could see you now, he'd be so proud."

Soon the car begins moving.

I twist around and watch through the back window as our old house vanishes.

86.

Our visits to the principal's office are starting to seem like a regular thing. The next morning, you're called in to see her again. By the time we arrive, Anni and Ryan are already there.

"What am I going to do with the three of you?" She sighs. "First the fighting. Then the mice. And now *this*? Sneaking out of detention?"

"It was my fault," you say quickly. "I snuck out first. Anni and Ryan were just worried about me. That's the only reason they—"

Principal Carter cuts you off. "I don't want to hear whose fault it was. There are rules. And the three of you broke those rules. Although . . . it apparently took a while for Coach Markey to notice the room was empty."

Was that a smile on Principal Carter's face? It's tough to tell. But there's definitely something in her eyes. Something that makes me think she isn't quite as angry as she sounds.

"Five more days." She nods firmly. "That's your punishment. Another week of detention. *With* Coach Markey."

There it is again. That almost-smile.

I notice the same look on your face. You're excited about the punishment. You just don't want Principal Carter to know that.

"That's not all, though." Her gaze lands on you. "Zach, do you remember the assignment I gave you a few days ago?"

"You asked me to do something creative." Your eyes brighten. "And I *did*, actually. I started drawing some pictures."

"They're really good!" Anni says.

Ryan crosses his arms. "The picture of the troll was kind of insulting."

Principal Carter raises an eyebrow. "You drew a troll?"

You nod. "And a spy. And also a knight."

"Well, I'm glad you took the assignment seriously," Principal Carter says. "Because I'm giving you another one. All three of you."

"What is it?"

"Do you know what the word *collaboration* means?"

Anni speaks up. "It's like, when people work together."

"Exactly. I'd like the three of you to collaborate on a story."

"What *kind* of story?" Ryan asks.

"That's up to you. It can be fiction or nonfiction. Funny or scary or sad. The only rule is, you have to each contribute."

She turns her attention in your direction. "And since you seem to enjoy drawing, maybe you can add some illustrations."

The three of you exchange looks.

Principal Carter pushes back her chair. "Well, then. You can get back to class now. And I'll look forward to reading your story at the end of next week."

87.

In detention, the three of you try to figure out what to write about.

"Whatever it is," you say, "there should be lots of action."

"But it also has to be funny," Ryan adds.

"And at some point, there should be a twist!" Anni drums the table excitedly. "Every story needs a big twist at the end!"

For the next few minutes, the three of you toss ideas back and forth. Eventually, the outline of a story begins to take shape.

Everyone decides the best way to write the story is by taking turns.

You volunteer to write the first part. Anni will take over after that. Then Ryan. From there—back to you.

I can see how excited you are about the project. So is Anni. But something's bothering Ryan. He stares down at the table, chewing his lip.

You've noticed too. "What's the matter?" you ask. "I thought you *wanted* to write something."

"I *do*." His words come in broken scraps. "It's just. I'm kinda worried. That my other friends—"

"Are gonna make fun of you for writing some silly story with a couple of nerds?" Anni guesses.

Ryan shrugs. "You know how people at school are. Everyone splits off into their ..."

"Cliques." You nod in recognition. "I know."

"I wish I was the kind of person who didn't care what anyone else thought." Ryan's hands clench into fists. "But I *do* care."

"So you don't want to write the story?" you ask.

"No, I think it'll be fun!" Ryan insists. "But maybe we can keep it a secret."

A light comes on behind Anni's eyes. And I know what flipped the switch. It was that last word Ryan spoke.

Secret.

She looks from you to Ryan like a superspy planning her next mission. "Don't worry. I have a plan."

88.

Once upon a time, there were three prisoners. A knight, a troll, and a spy from a faraway land. They were locked away in a deep, dark dungeon.

This is the beginning of the story. A story written by three authors, each taking turns, trading off writing duties. Sometimes, the work is done in detention. Other times, the story spills outside the walls of the school, into the authors' homes.

The story is written on sheets of paper. There are also illustrations.

Once a section is complete, the pages are folded into fourths and stashed away in the author's backpack until the perfect moment. When nobody's looking, the folded pages are slipped through a thin slot in a locker door.

This way, the collaboration stays a secret.

One story.

Three authors.

A couple of the authors have pointed out that this whole system is maybe more complicated than it needs to be. So many folded sheets of paper. So much sneaking around.

Couldn't they just share a Google Doc?

But they keep the system going because... Well, it's also kind of *fun*.

The story keeps growing and growing.

At first, the prisoners don't get along very well. Especially after the troll releases a horde of mutant mice inside the dungeon. But after the knight and the spy take revenge, an unlikely friendship is formed.

The story is packed with goofy humor and exciting action.

A knight who goes missing.

A daring dungeon escape.

A terrible injury in the middle of spooky ruins.

Just when it looks like the knight is doomed...

The spy and the troll arrive.

And they're driving a giant monster truck. *With* floaties for wheels.

Just like Anni said. Every story needs a big twist ending!

89.

I've faded away to almost nothing.

Your real life is crowding me out. School's getting busier. You're spending more time with Anni and Ryan. And of course, there's the story. A smile splashes across your face whenever you open your locker and—*surprise!*—a few folded sheets of paper are waiting for you.

These days, I see your life in glimpses. Moments come and go.

I watch you at the table with your mom, eating dinner. You've started something new lately. While you eat, you and your mom will tell stories. But these aren't stories about an imaginary world. There are no knights or monsters.

These are stories about your dad.

How he met your mom. How he used to throw you into the air, so high you thought you might keep right on going.

Through the clouds. Into space. How his sneezes seemed to shake the entire house. How he let you paint one of his miniatures.

The stories always make us smile.

Even when they make us sad.

Another moment, another glimpse.

I see you inside your room, at your desk. Hunched over a sheet of paper with a pencil in your hand.

On a shelf nearby, the little plastic knight is in its usual place. But it's no longer alone. Now it's joined by a bunch of other fantasy characters. Unearthed after all these years, cleaned off, and displayed proudly on your bookcase.

A drawing takes shape on the paper.

A giant, standing taller than the buildings and trees all around her. There's something familiar about that almost-smile on her face.

I blink and the moment is gone.

Replaced by another.

We're in Principal Carter's office. Ryan and Anni are here with us. Anni plops something down on the principal's desk. A stack of paper, held together by a rubber band. The cover reads:

THE THREE PRISONERS
Based on a True Story
(Sort Of)

By
ZACH BELVIN
ANNI LAI
RYAN ATKINSON

"Here's the assignment you asked us to do," Anni says.

Principal Carter picks the clump of pages off her desk. "I'm looking forward to reading it."

"Ooh, almost forgot!" You lean down, unzipping your backpack and reaching inside. "I added one more illustration last night."

"You did?" Ryan sounds surprised.

"I got inspired."

You slide a page across the desk. The giant with the almost-smile and the familiar face.

Your eyes move from the giant on the page to the giant on the other side of the desk. "Thank you. For, you know, *everything.*"

Principal Carter smiles. And this time, there's no *almost* about it.

The moment dims.

And suddenly, we're in a crowded hall. You turn a corner and nearly collide with the Matts. They're back from suspension. You try to step around them, but they move into your path.

Matt #1 smirks down at you. "Didja miss us?"

Matt #2 glances around. "Where's your imaginary buddy?"

People are starting to look. A crowd is beginning to form around you and the Matts, everyone wondering if there's about to be a rematch.

Then a voice calls out from a nearby locker.

"Hey, Matt! Come here!"

Both Matts turn and see Ryan. He waves them over.

Matt #1 calls back. "Dude, we're kinda in the middle of something!" As if picking on you is on their to-do list.

"Just get over here!" Ryan yells.

The Matts exchange a shrug before turning and stalking away.

Ryan nods at you quickly. Then his arms are on the Matts' shoulders, leading them in the other direction.

In each of these glimpses, the world around me seems to dim just a little more. Voices are muffled. Colors are less colorful.

Of course, it's not the world that's fading.

It's *me*.

My expiration date could come any minute now. I've always known this was how my story was going to end.

Except.

There's one thing I forgot. Something Anni said back in detention.

Every good story should have a big twist ending.

90.

It's impossible to say what day it is. They all run together now.

We're in the garage. You're looking up at the pegboard on the wall. The tools are all hanging exactly where they're supposed to be.

You reach up and grab one.

CLANG! The tool lands in a basket that's attached to the front of your bike. On the pegboard, the only trace of the missing tool is the outline of a shovel.

The moment flickers away. Another takes its place.

We're on the sidewalk outside your house. Your *old* house. Our first time back since you dug up the box.

You climb off your bike.

"What're we doing here?" I glance at the shovel in the basket. "You planning on doing some more digging?"

You don't answer. Which isn't much of a surprise, I guess. These days, I doubt you realize I'm even *here*.

There are people in the front yard of your old house. The little girl and her dads. The last time we saw them, we were sitting in Ryan's yard. Here they are again, kicking a soccer ball back and forth between them.

I'm surprised when you wave to them. And even more surprised when you call out, "Hi. This might sound really weird, but...uh...I actually used to live here."

You point to our old house.

Which is now *their* house.

But if they find any of this weird, they don't show it. The game of soccer is put on hold. The girl races in your direction, trailed by her dads.

"You really used to live here?" the girl asks.

You nod. "It was a long time ago though. Probably even before you were born."

"Wow!" She's clearly impressed.

"Where do you live now?" her dad asks.

"On the other side of town. Not too far by bike." You tap your handlebar. Then your eyes move to the basket. And the shovel. "When I was still living here, I buried something in the backyard."

The girl's eyes go wide. "Like *treasure*?"

"Kind of."

"Cool!" She hops up and down. "There's buried treasure in our backyard!"

"Actually…" You shift nervously from foot to foot. "I sort of dug it up."

"Zach!" There's an edge to my voice. "I'm pretty sure you're about to confess to a crime."

Once again, you ignore me.

You look from the girl to her dads. "I came here because… I wanted to apologize. A couple of weeks ago, I snuck into your backyard while you were away. And I dug up the thing that was there. I totally get it if you're mad. I should've asked first, and I'm really sorry."

The two men exchange a glance. Then their attention lands on you again.

"This thing you buried," one of them says. "It must've been really important to you if you came back to dig it up after all this time."

The girl tugs at her dad's sleeve. "Of *course* it was important! It was *treasure!*"

"I didn't realize *how* important it was," you explain. "Not for a long time. I'm glad to have it back. But I'm sorry I didn't get permission first."

"We appreciate that," her dad says.

"Also…um…I kind of forgot to fill in the hole after I was done. *Lots* of holes, actually. It took me a few tries to find what I was looking for." Your eyes land on the shovel again. "I can fill them in now, if you want."

"That's so nice of you to offer," one of her dads says.

"But we already filled in the holes," the other says.

You blink with surprise. "*Really?*"

He nods. "We noticed them in a corner of the backyard. Behind some bushes."

"We thought some kind of rodent must've made them," says the other dad. "It's actually a relief to find out it was you."

"Oh. Good." You grip the handlebar tighter. You're about to climb onto the bike when the little girl speaks up again.

"Did you like living in my house?" she asks. "I mean— *before* it was my house?"

You think about this. "I was really lucky to grow up there."

"Did you have any friends nearby?"

"Actually, yeah." You point to Ryan's house. "My best friend lived next door. He still lives there, actually."

"Are you still friends?"

If she'd asked you this question at the beginning of the school year, you would've had a different answer. But now, you nod. "Yeah. We are."

"I wish *I* had a friend next door." The girl gives the sidewalk a sullen kick. "There aren't any other kids my age on the *whole street.*"

You give the girl a sympathetic look. Then your expression changes. An idea flickers in your eyes. "You know, I actually had *another* friend."

You turn to look at me. The first time you've looked at me in weeks.

"This friend was ... different," you say.

"Different how?"

"Well, to start off with, he was made out of fur. *Purple* fur."

The girl raises her eyebrows. "Purple fur?"

"That's right." You hold your hand next to the top of my head. "He was *this tall*. And he was as round as that soccer ball you were kicking."

A suspicious look comes over the girl's face. She glances at her dads. They just shrug.

Her doubtful gaze lands on you again. "Are you making this up?"

You shake your head. "I can prove it."

"How?"

"See for yourself." You gesture in my direction. "He's standing right next to me."

The girl's head turns. And then the strangest thing happens.

She actually seems to be looking at me.

Not *through* me. Or *past* me. Or *near* me.

Right *at* me.

91.

Maybe it's just a coincidence. Maybe the girl isn't seeing anything except empty air. But that doesn't explain the other totally weird thing that just happened.

When I look down at myself, I see...

Myself.

Again.

Not the faded version.

I see *all of me.*

And so—it seems—does the girl.

"There he is!" She hops up and down. "I *see* him!"

"You *do*?" her dad says, surprised.

"Of course!" The girl points at me. "He's right here! And he's supercute!"

My head is spinning. From the moment I blinked into existence, I've been invisible to everyone except you. And now, out of nowhere, someone else can see me! And she thinks I'm *cute*!

"Ah, right," her dad says. "*Now* I see who you're talking about."

But his eyes are off by about a foot. He doesn't see me. Not like the girl.

"His name's Shovel," you say.

The girl's gaze moves from me to the basket on the front of your bike. "Like *that* shovel?"

"Yep."

"That's a funny name."

"He's a funny guy."

She takes a step toward me. "Nice to meet you, Shovel. My name's Rose."

"Um. Hi, Rose." I give her an awkward wave.

"Me and Shovel have had all sorts of adventures together." You crouch down, so you're closer to Rose's level. And *my* level. "Do you wanna know the best thing about being friends with Shovel?"

"What?"

"He's always there when you need him. No matter what. If you're bored. Or lonely. Or just want someone to talk to. Shovel's there. I'm really lucky I had a friend like him for so long."

When you say this last part, your eyes are on me. There's a happy-sad smile on your face.

You turn back to Rose. "Oh, and I forgot to mention—he's an amazing juggler."

"Do you think…" She shifts from foot to foot. "I can be friends with Shovel too?"

"I don't know," you say seriously. "You should probably ask your parents."

Rose spins. "Can me and Shovel be friends?"

They trade a look and a private smile. Then their attention lands on the girl again.

"Sure, button," says one.

The other nods. "You can be friends with Shovel."

She looks to me. "Um, Shovel?"

"Yeah?" I say.

"Do you maybe wanna be friends?"

My fur brims with nervous excitement. It's been years since anyone asked me something like that. The last time was you. I didn't think it'd ever happen again.

A smile spreads across my face. "That'd be great!"

"Yaaay!" Rose performs a little dance, right there on the sidewalk. "Can we play right now?"

I start to answer, but then…

A thread of uncertainty pulls at me. When I look at you, I see the same thing in your face.

It's not easy letting go.

"You sure you're okay with this, Zach?" I say. "Because if not—"

"I think it's a great idea." The slightest tremble in your

voice. A tiny scrap of sorrow in your smile. "You two are gonna have so much fun together."

Rose cheers again. She grabs her dads' hands and pulls them across the yard, in the direction of their house.

Which used to be *our* house.

Halfway across the yard, she looks over her shoulder at me. "Aren't you coming, Shovel?"

But something holds me in place, here on the sidewalk. You're still crouched beside me.

It's true what you said earlier. We've had some incredible adventures together. And you still have so much to look forward to. The real world is a huge place, full of happiness and heartbreak, beautiful sights and scary monsters. But I know you can handle it. You're the bravest hero I've ever met.

"Goodbye, Zach," I say.

Your eyes shine. "Goodbye, Shovel."

I watch you climb onto your bike and ride away down the street.

And then I'm running, chasing after Rose. She squeals with happiness. My legs are no longer weak. I feel like I can run for miles and miles.

92.

Everything is new and old. Everything is strange and familiar.

When I'm with Rose, it reminds me of BEFORE. Back when you were younger and your life wasn't so crowded. Rose doesn't have as many distractions. The constant pull of homework and devices and after-school activities. Things are like they used to be with you.

But also different.

Rose isn't interested in castles and kingdoms. But she's obsessed with outer space. When she climbs onto her tire swing, it transforms into a rocket ship. And when she hops off again, her feet touch down on another planet. The ground is pale blue and crawling with alien creatures.

That first day, we must've explored half the galaxy together. All before dinnertime.

Her room is your old room. Stepping through the

doorway for the first time, memories wash over me like a wave. It's been so long since I was here.

But now, the place has changed. The walls are another color. The bed has migrated to a different part of the room. The toys spilling out of the closet aren't yours.

New and old.

Strange and familiar.

I'm still standing at the edge of your room (*which is no longer your room*), looking at the things around me (*someone else's things*), when all of a sudden—

An extraterrestrial monster bursts through the door.

The hulking creature rampages across the floor. It launches into the air, all claws and teeth. Before I have time to respond, the enormous beast pounces on Rose.

And starts licking her face.

She's laughing and rolling around on the floor. The terrifying alien has become a drooling golden retriever.

Rose takes me everywhere with her. To the dinner table with her dads. To other planets. And to preschool.

When I arrive at her school for the first time, I look around at all the bright colors. Other kids are running around, wild and happy. The air is filled with laughter and music. And best of all...

I'm not the only imaginary friend.

Not even close.

Practically everyone has an imaginary friend. Everyone *her* age anyway.

There's a striped kangaroo with a magical pouch.

And a Slinky, who has a habit of breaking into song.

And a lawn gnome on a skateboard.

It's a strange crowd.

I fit right in.

93.

Days slip into weeks.

Weeks melt into months.

Life with Rose is never boring. Today we're in her front yard. Except it's *not* her front yard.

It's Blargon!

For those who've never visited, Blargon is an extremely dangerous planet, exactly 10.2 bazillion light-years from Earth and crawling with deadly monsters.

Right now, we're jumping back and forth through the sprinkler. Except it's *not* the sprinkler.

It's a Blargonian snake monster!

The creature spits venom into the air. If we want to survive, we'll have to leap through the poisonous spray before it comes raining down on us.

We're doing our best to avoid being vaporized by Blargonian snake venom when a familiar voice calls out.

"Hi, Rose!"

I blink and the alien planet disappears.

We're back in the front yard.

The voice came from next door. I look in that direction. Standing in front of Ryan's house, smiling in our direction...

It's *you.*

You're taller. Your shoulders are broader. More than ever, you remind me of your dad.

You're not alone. Anni is there next to you. The front door opens and Ryan steps outside. He gives you and Anni a double fist bump.

Rose waves to you. "Guess what! We went to Blargon!"

"What's Blargon?" you call back.

She shakes her head at your cluelessness. "It's another planet!"

You slap your forehead, like *duh.* "Oh, right. *Now* I remember!"

"Shovel's here too." Rose points to me.

You smile. "Hi, Shovel!"

My name. Your voice. Hearing it makes me feel warm all over. Even if your eyes are looking somewhere else. At a spot on the ground that's almost (*but not quite*) where I'm standing.

A moment later, you and Anni follow Ryan into his house.

But by then, Rose and I are back on Blargon.

94.

A butterfly flaps its wings.

An elephant farts.

One little moment in time changes everything.

I used to look back at your life—at *our* life—and wonder: What would I change? How would things be different?

I'm done thinking that way now.

No matter how much we might want to, we can't change the past. All we can do is try to learn from it. To make the most of the time we have here. To appreciate the people around us. Our family and our friends.

Even the *imaginary* ones.

From now on, I'm okay with the butterfly flapping its wings. I say, *Go ahead, elephant. Let it rip.*

95.

I've always wondered what happens to imaginary friends when we reach our expiration date. Even though I still haven't reached mine, I think I understand:

Nothing lasts forever. People die. Imaginary friends fade.

But that doesn't mean they're gone.

Even after someone or something goes away, a part of them still remains. In the memories you keep. In the stories you tell around the dinner table and slip through locker doors.

In this way, I'm still a part of you.

And so is your dad.

We were there BEFORE.

And our light shines on AFTER.

All you have to do is remember.

Author's Note

I wrote IMAGINARY three times.

The first attempt was years ago. When the book was complete, I didn't try to get it published. On a gut level, I knew the book wasn't ready. Or perhaps *I* was the one who wasn't ready.

You might be wondering: How did I know this? The answer is: I just *did*. It was like trying on a pair of shoes. Maybe you think they look incredibly cool. Maybe you've been wanting them for months. But as soon as your feet slide inside, you can just tell.

The shoes aren't right.

And my book wasn't right either.

Years went by. Other books were written and published. But the idea for *Imaginary* stayed with me. Drifting in a corner of my mind like an imaginary ball of purple fur, popping up to catch my attention from time to time, saying, "Hi there, remember me?"

I *did* remember it. I couldn't get it out of my head. And eventually, I decided to take another crack at it. A new version. A complete rewrite. I made a return trip to the world I had created years earlier, enjoying the chance to revisit the familiar characters and places. But just like before: When it was done, I left the file on my hard drive, unpublished.

My weird story about an imaginary friend still wasn't ready.

More time went by. More books were written. But like before, the pesky idea wouldn't leave me alone. Eventually, I went back to it. Again. A complete rewrite. And this time, when I finished...

The shoes fit!

Finally!

The book felt ready. Even though so many elements had changed over time, the basic idea remained the same: It was the story of two friends. One real and one imaginary. Narrated by the imaginary friend. It was a story about imagination and grief, about escape and acceptance.

I stuck with *Imaginary* all these years. Just like Shovel stuck with Zach. No matter how many times I abandoned this story, it wouldn't abandon *me*. This was a story I had to tell.

Even if I didn't tell it right the first time.

Or the time after that.

I got there eventually.

Acknowledgments

Thank you to my wise and generous agent, Sarah Burnes. For encouraging me to stick with this strange story through the years. For reading multiple drafts, even though each version was basically a whole new book. And for helping me narrow my focus to the parts that really mattered.

And huge thanks to everyone else at The Gernert Company, in particular Sophie Pugh-Sellers, Will Roberts, and Rebecca Gardner.

I'm incredibly grateful to have Maggie Lehrman as an editor. Our collaboration now includes *two* books with unconventional narrators. First, a robot. Now, an imaginary friend. But in each case, you've helped me to find the humanity in these unhuman characters.

Thanks also to the amazing team at Abrams: Emily Daluga, Brooke Shearouse, Nicole Schaefer, Jenny Choy,

Trish McNamara-O'Neill, Megan Evans, and Andrew Smith, as well as the exceptionally perceptive copyeditors and proofreaders who carefully read through this book, caught errors big and small, and generally made me seem smarter than I actually am.

Jason Richman at UTA remains my man in Hollywood. Thanks for everything you've done, Jason!

In *Imaginary*, Zach deals with the loss of a parent: a tragedy that is incredibly painful and difficult for anyone, *especially* young people. Paula Marchese read an early draft of this book, offering her professional expertise and insight into these issues. In addition, she gave me the line, "*A shovel is also a tool*," which I loved so much, I stole it! Principal Carter uses these exact words in one of her conversations with Zach. Thank you, Paula!

And thanks also to Paula's daughter, Siena, who was the first *actual kid* to read *Imaginary*, and who offered many valuable insights of her own.

I would like to thank my family on both sides of the Atlantic. To my mom and dad, as well as aunts and uncles and cousins: I'm incredibly grateful to have such a wonderful network of support and love. Und auch meine deutsche Familie, Michael und Irmtrud Schlör, Zenta Englert, Karin und Kalle und Oskar: Ich bin sehr glücklich (in beiden

Sinnen des Wortes: fortunate and happy!) ein Teil eurer Familie zu sein!

I write this during a pandemic, a time when none of us can see each other in real life. I'm sure everyone reading this can relate. This difficult period has shown the huge and vital importance of family, friends, and community. Hopefully, by the time this book has been published, we'll all be able to see each other again—*without* screens!

And of course: Eva. My best friend, my favorite dinner companion and trusted consultant on things both huge and trivial, my earliest reader, my tech consultant, and my wife.

During the process of writing this book, we added one more member to the Bacon family . . . Our daughter, Clara! To whom this book is dedicated! Clara, I look forward to watching you grow up, to finding out what kind of a person you'll become, to the imaginary adventures you dream up inside that head of yours.

This book deals with a death in the family. Three years ago, my family experienced our own loss: the death of my brother, Evan Bacon. It was the most difficult and painful thing I've ever been through. I thought about Evan many times during the writing of *Imaginary*. Memories that were both happy and sad, like Zach's memories of his father. Memories that I will always carry with me.

This is a book of fiction, but some parts are also true. Including the words that come at the very end: *"Even after someone or something goes away, a part of them still remains…All you have to do is remember."*

I'll always remember you, Evan.